Mark D'Arbanville is the author of over thirty books of fiction and non-fiction, which have been published in Australia, UK and the USA and translated into sixteen languages. He was born and grew up in London and now lives in Australia. This is Mark D'Arbanville's second contemporary novel. He writes other works of fiction as Colin Falconer.

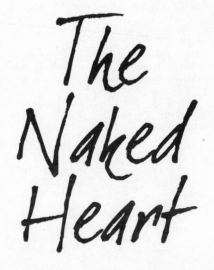

The Naked Heart

Mark D'Arbanville

BANTAM
SYDNEY AUCKLAND TORONTO NEW YORK LONDON

THE NAKED HEART
A BANTAM BOOK

First published in Australia and New Zealand in 2005 by Bantam

National Library of Australia
Cataloguing-in-Publication Entry

D'Arbanville, Mark.
The naked heart.

ISBN 1 86325 497 8.

I. Title.

A823.4

Transworld Publishers,
a division of Random House Australia Pty Ltd
20 Alfred Street, Milsons Point, NSW 2061
http://www.randomhouse.com.au

Random House New Zealand Limited
18 Poland Road, Glenfield, Auckland

Transworld Publishers,
a division of The Random House Group Ltd
61-63 Uxbridge Road, London W5 5SA

Random House Inc
1745 Broadway, New York, New York 10036

Cover and internal design: sasocontent & design
Cover image: Getty Images
Typeset by Midland Typesetters, Maryborough, Victoria
Printed and bound by Griffin Press, Netley, South Australia

10 9 8 7 6 5 4 3 2 1

I wrote this for the Butterfly
and for carpe diem.

Prologue

Muxia, Galicia, Spain

Iglesia de Santa María de la Barca

Father Diego Calderón found the photograph when he was cleaning the church in preparation for the Easter festival. It was a black and white photograph of a young girl, perhaps seven or eight years old. It had been sealed in a plastic cover and must have been there for some time. On the reverse was a typewritten prayer.

Father Diego knew a little English and the rest he translated that night in his study, working slowly but diligently by the light of his desk lamp. Outside his window, the Atlantic beat on the rocks below the church, just a hundred yards away. Two thousand years before, the Virgin had landed here in Galicia in a stone boat, or so legend said.

He felt deeply moved by what he read. He had been a priest now for thirty years but had never failed to be touched by the frailties and complexities of the human condition. Life was full of poignant tragedies and quiet desperation and exhilarating triumphs. In the rites of birth, marriage and death he heard the beating of the divine heart.

He wondered how the prayer had come to be in this place, for few souls ever came this far along the camino. He did not sleep well that night.

The next morning he replaced the prayer beneath the pedestal of the Virgin and, having done so, said a prayer for the young girl in the photograph. He wondered if she was a woman now, for the photograph was a grainy monochrome and looked to be twenty or thirty years old. He spoke also a prayer for the hand that had left her plea there in his church, to the tender mercy of the Madonna.

The words to the prayer were quite beautiful, the work of an educated, perhaps poetic hand. It vexed him that he would never know how the prayer came to be here in his little church. He would have liked to know the story behind it.

But he supposed he never would.

Mark D'Arbanville

One

I open my eyes to a pale blue sky. I am floating high above the trees. It feels warm, there is no pain, and there is light. I sink into a cherry gelatin cloud. I could stay here forever.

– Anna? Anna, can you hear me?

There are voices intruding on my opiate silence, and they get louder and more painful. The lightness is slipping away and I know I must come back, down from these clouds and the sweeping sky. There is a dull ache in my head. I am too heavy to fly now.

I reach out a hand, but the clouds slip through my fingers and I know I have to return.

Not yet.

But it is too late.

Faces crowd in. So many voices, too many. I don't know who is calling to me, I don't want to be here, I never wanted to come back, why am I back here? A strong and sterile smell.

I open my eyes. There are alarms going off and someone is screaming for a nurse, a doctor, and I feel a rush of panic.

Where am I?

I take a breath and scream. I feel a needle inserted in my arm.

I don't want to be here. I want them all to go away.

Mark D'Arbanville

Two

Navarre, Spain: between Pamplona and Puente la Reina

Madeleine is sitting on a low brick wall next to the fountain. The village is deserted for siesta; it looks like the set of a spaghetti western. The plaza is empty save for a dog asleep next to a bright blue Pepsi dispensing machine, and an old woman dressed entirely in black who is sitting outside her house with her legs apart reading a John Grisham novel.

Mark's first words to Madeleine charm her and sweep her off her feet.

— It's hot.

Her eyes speculate. She is wearing a sassy little brimmed hat with a long yellow ribbon. He cannot see her face under the brim.

— Where have you walked from? she asks.

— Roncesvalles. You?

– Jean Pierre Pied de Port.

– American?

– Boston. But I work in London.

– I'm from England.

– I thought so. Love the accent.

– Thanks. Saw it in a shop. Paid a lot of money for it.

They walk together for a while. She has come to the *camino*, she says, to look for something but she doesn't know what. There is something missing in her life. But of course. People walk the *camino*, the ancient pilgrimage trail between the Pyrenees and the Spanish Atlantic coast, for many reasons. The reasons are often spiritual, but not always religious.

– What about you?

There are a number of answers he can give. He can lie, for instance, and say he came for spiritual renewal. Or he can tell her a version of the truth; that always works well.

– It's my honeymoon.

– Where's your wife?

– Greece.

– Very romantic. You both need a lot of personal space?

– She's not my wife. We didn't get married.

– Cold feet?

– Hot head. So I came here. I wanted to be alone for a while.

She is quiet for a long time. It's a long climb through fields of sunflowers and asparagus. Huge white windmills dominate the ridge, the blades sweeping and moaning.

She stops to drink from her water bottle. Fields of gold and green stretch all the way back to Pamplona. He can see it in her face: *better stay away from this one.*

Mark D'Arbanville

When they reach the top of the pass she stops to talk to three other guys, students from Canada. He walks on.

He scares people. In lots of ways. He has a past, a scary past, and ghosts behind his eyes. He has come to realise that he is charming, witty and very, very scary.

But then the real reason he is there is lying in a hospital bed in south west London. The force of his feelings had scared him as much as it had scared everyone around him. If he hadn't fallen so chaotically in love, he doubted that the need for a spiritual renewal would ever have occurred to him.

Three

I can hear voices, dull and hushed. They will not let me hide. Finally I open my eyes.

– Anna? Anna, can you hear me? Squeeze my hand if you can hear me.

It takes some time but finally I manage what he asks.

– Anna, do you know where you are?

I shake my head.

– My name is Doctor Maddison. You are in Hammersmith hospital. You were in a car accident.

The voice drones on. I watch his face. His eyes are blinking rapidly. He looks very tired. There is another doctor with a chart, making notes.

– Anna, do you have any pain?

I try to answer, but my throat feels like there is a razor blade lodged in it. I feel scared, very scared.

Dr Maddison picks up my hand from the bed. His feels strong and very warm. His eyes are an intense blue, the blue

Mark D'Arbanville

of sky, and I want to go back there, back to the sky. I try to swim to his eyes. My head rises a fraction from the pillow but I am chained again to the earth.

– Anna, it's going to be all right. There are many people who love you and want you to get better. You do want to get better?

I squeeze his hand again. I never want to let go. I feel so alone and so afraid.

I always have.

Four

The family are waiting in an anteroom by the nurses' station.

— Sometimes, the doctor is saying, with a severe head trauma, there can be deficits.

— Deficits? Anna's father asks. What does that mean?

— She may have impaired neurological function.

Her father is still at a loss.

— He means, her sister says, that she could be a vegetable.

There is silence.

— Sometimes what may be classified as a minor brain injury may result in significant impairment which may affect a person's life permanently, while a person who has suffered a severe injury may be able to return to a life that is close to the one they had before the accident. She is emerging now, and we will run some tests, check her motor responses. You must be patient.

— Will she not recognise us? her husband asks.

– I don't know. The brain is a fragile organ. There is often memory loss to some degree. This may only be temporary.

– But she will be all right?

He turns to face Anna's mother. For almost three months she has come each day to the hospital, and had begun to give up hope.

– The insult to the brain was severe and diffuse. Her recovery is uncertain. She could make a full recovery, with luck, or she may stay as she is.

– A vegetable, her sister Cathy repeats.

– With severe deficits, the doctor says. He takes a breath. We will have to wait and see. That is the most accurate answer I can give you.

Her husband sits down with his head in his hands. Anna's mother is pulling at a paper tissue, little pieces fluttering to the floor like feathers from a wounded and struggling bird.

– Can we see her? he asks.

– Anna is very disoriented. She doesn't remember anything at this stage. Perhaps tomorrow.

Anna's father looks at his wife, then at the others. He shakes his head. He always knew it might end this way.

Five

Flowers fill the room. And there are cards, cards from people I don't remember. Someone has propped a pinboard of photographs on a chair beside the bed. My fingers trace the faces in the pictures. These strangers are the people I am supposed to love.

My heart starts racing and I can't breathe. The feeling of panic is so intense I have to close my eyes. What if I never remember?

There is a small compact on the bedside table and I flip it open. Who is this woman in the mirror? Her hair is short, there is no make-up. A stranger like the people in the photographs.

Bright blue eyes but what lies inside them?

What has she seen and what does she know that I don't?

– So you're Anna, I say to the face in the mirror. My hands start to shake and I drop the compact on the floor. I remember what I had for breakfast. I remember how warm the neurologist's hand felt on mine.

And nothing else.

Mark D'Arbanville

Six

Carrión de los Condes, Castille

– **Holy fuck, look at your feet.** What the?

Mark looks up. It's Madeleine. He has not seen her since Pamplona.

– Got a few blisters going on.

– They look like raw steak.

She fetches a first aid kit from her backpack and kneels down.

– What are you doing?

– I'm a nurse. Specialised in paediatrics. But I can patch up feet too.

She pricks the blisters with a sterile needle and cleans and dresses the ones that have already burst on the back of his heels. He is touched. There is something intimate and also humbling about someone tending your feet. She tears off a strip of leukoplast with her teeth.

– How's the honeymoon coming along?

– I've had better.

– How many honeymoons have you had?

She has a playful smile. He is intrigued. She says fuck, nurses children and has an Ayn Rand paperback in her backpack. And she is flirting with him.

– You want to go for a drink? he asks her.

– Okay, but I'm not going to marry you.

– Shit. So what am I going to do with these seven days on Santorini?

– You don't have to marry someone to sleep with them.

– Ah, that may have been what I've been doing wrong.

– It makes one night stands very expensive.

They walk into town from the albergue and find a bar in one of the narrow cobbled streets of the old city. He orders a bottle of cheap red wine. The town is full of tourists and Spaniards dressed up in medieval costume for a festival. They find a seat at the bar between a Castilian maiden and a Moorish knight with a curved scimitar in his belt.

– So. Stop being so mysterious. What happened to you?

– What do you mean?

– You twitch, you never rest. You constantly get these looks on your face, you sigh, you talk to yourself.

– Christ, am I that bad? Maybe I should be in a locked ward.

– I've seen homeless with more inner peace.

A long silence.

– So what happened, Mark? Do you want to tell me?

He tells her his story in a monotone. He is tired of it now. He wishes it had happened to someone else. It scares people

Mark D'Arbanville

and they make an excuse to go the bathroom and never come back. But he was never a very good liar, except when he had to tell the truth to someone he loved. So the scary man tells her his story, from the affair with Anna, to the moving on, and the desperate engagement to Siobhan. But he doesn't tell her everything. He had sworn not to.

– So what happened to what's her name?

– Siobhan? She decided not to show up.

– At the wedding?

– Uh-huh.

Madeleine finds this hilarious.

– Thanks for your sensitivity.

– It would never have worked. You're lucky. What did the guests say?

– There weren't that many. Some of them even seemed to understand. They helped me drink the champagne.

– How did she do it?

– She sent me a text message. It said: *Got scared. Have gone to Greece. I am so sorry. Siobhan.*

– You're kidding.

– She was smarter than me. Like you said. She worked out that it probably wouldn't have lasted.

– Well, you were only going out for a few months. And all that time your real girlfriend was in a coma.

– We were both on the rebound, I guess.

– Rebound? You were both pinging around like pinballs.

– That's apparent now. It wasn't then.

– What did you do? When she didn't show?

– I spent my wedding night holed up in a bar in a sleazy

neck of the city, with my best man. I drank bourbon till three in the morning.

– What would you have done it if she had turned up?

– Probably the same thing.

– Probably.

He likes Madeleine. She has some rock and roll in her, and a cute smile. Just what a very angry man who is bitterly and mortally hurt is looking for. They drink the bottle of wine and then another one, and talk about art, philosophy, literature and blisters.

That night he does not sleep with her and she does not sleep with him. They go back to their pilgrim dormitories in the albergue and he wonders if they will see each other during the walk the next day but leaves it to fate to decide.

And he goes to bed promising himself he won't think about Anna, just for once, just for the sake of fucking principle.

But of course he does.

Mark D'Arbanville

Seven

So many people, the people that I love, all of them complete strangers.

A woman who says she is my mother, sobbing so hard she can barely breathe. Her eyes look the same as mine. I feel her tears fall on my face and her arms around my shoulders and I wonder if I loved her, I wonder if we were close.

I have a sister, Cathy. And I am married. My husband sits now at the side of my bed, choked with tears. They tell me he has not slept in a bed for weeks and stayed at the hospital every night. They tell me his name is Paul.

– Anna, Anna thank God. Anna, you came back to us, baby.

Paul has gentle brown eyes. I wonder how long we have been married. I ask him questions and he eagerly fills in details.

– Were we happy?

He seems confused by the question.

– We were like every married couple. We had some problems but, yes, we were incredibly happy. You are wonderful, Anna. I love you very much. I thought I was going to lose you. I couldn't stand the thought of losing you. I don't know what I'd do without you.

He squeezes my hand so hard that it hurts.

– Can you remember anything about me, Anna?

His eyes are so eager and so desperate. I want to think of something, give him something.

– I remember your hands, sweetheart.

And then he is hugging me again. I wonder if he did this before. It is hard to breathe. I am not sure whether I can cope if he is always like this.

The doctor comes in and says, your wife needs her rest, and he hugs me again and leaves. I hear him shouting to someone as he leaves the room:

– She remembers my hands! She remembers my hands!

I experience a sense of foreboding. Must I give all of these people something, some reward, pretend I remember when I really don't? I feel tired and confused. Paul seems nice and very attractive and yet I know nothing about him.

I am a blank slate. Already hands are frantically scribbling their names on me. I feel violated; I want them all to go away. I want to be clean and fresh and new.

Mark D'Arbanville

Eight

Strange dreams, nightmares stalking my sleep like thieves.

The nurses tell me they found me sleepwalking in the corridor and had to take me back to bed. And now this morning there is another face leaning over the bed, a woman's face.

– Hi, Anna. Do you remember me? It's Sally.

I search the woman's face for something that is familiar but there is nothing. I smile at her, hoping to soften the blow of my amnesia.

– I'm sorry. I don't remember you.

– I know. Don't worry.

– Who are you?

– I was a friend. We worked together. She hesitates, uncertain. I brought you this.

She hands me a photograph album. It is black and heavy and has sharp edges. There is a rose on the front, gold embossed.

– What is this?

– I made this for you. There are photographs, places we have gone together, some emails and letters you sent me. I thought it might help.

I love her immediately. I have a sense of her, even without memory. I feel safe. She hugs me gently, not like Paul, and I do not want to let her go.

Sally talks me through the book of memories. It is like prying into someone else's private life.

– I met my husband yesterday, I tell her.

A shadow passes across her face, like a cloud over the sun.

– He seems like a good man, a kind man. Do you know him well?

– Of course, Anna, he's great.

But now her smile is not so open. She has brought me photographs and stories of my life and now there is something she is not telling me. I want to press her but another part of me draws back. I want to wake to a fairy story. So far, they have told me I am a princess. Where is my happy ending?

Sally leaves and I pick up the book again and leaf through it. The emails are funny and smart. There are photographs of myself with Sally at luncheons, drinking champagne, on a beach somewhere, in bikinis. It seems we had some wonderful times together.

My fingers trace the contours of a photograph at the back of the book, Sally, me and a man. I find myself drawn to it. All the other photographs have captions except this one . . . who is he? I wonder. Perhaps a friend of Paul's. Sally will remember.

Mark D'Arbanville

Remember.

If I don't remember anything, will I still be me?

Who am I anyway? Am I the clean slate or the things that people choose to write upon it?

There is a strange feeling inside when I look at the face of the man in the photograph, a physical reaction that is unexpected and even a little embarrassing. I must ask Paul about this.

Or perhaps not.

Nine

Terradillos de los Templarios

Mark hears the echo of the heavy oak door and knows there is someone else in the church. It was built by the Templars in the eleventh century and so there is a false altar, and the shrine of the Madonna is set behind it, where the gloom of the apse is lit by votive candles.

He rises guiltily from his knees and hides the prayer and black and white photograph in his money belt. He never lets anyone see what he is doing.

 – I didn't pick you for a God botherer, Madeleine says.

 – Really? Even though we're on a pilgrimage?

 – What have you got there? You look guilty.

 – It's a prayer. I'm carrying it for a friend.

 – For fertility and a faithful husband?

 He looks away. It is what he would like to pray for her, if he were different, or if the situation were. It had been written long ago, before the smash of metal and glass and the wail of sirens on the Fulham Palace Road.

She kneels down also. The altar does not boast a particularly pious Madonna. She has no child and there is a lightness and flirtatiousness to her not always found in Catholic iconography. Is she Mary, Jesus' mother, or is she the Magdalen, or is she someone else? It's never clear. Not that it really matters.

– You like the Virgin? she asks him.

He doesn't know how to answer. He doesn't know what he expects to find here.

– In Roman days a Virgin was not . . . a virgin. She was a woman who didn't belong to a particular man, a priestess in one of the temples to Astarte or Venus. It didn't mean she didn't have sex. Quite the opposite. You know the Magdalen was a Virgin? Mary may have been too. The mother of Jesus was a priestess in a pagan temple.

– Did you just make that up to shock me?

– You paid your money to the Temple and then you made love to one of the priestesses. It was a sacred act.

– How do you know all this?

She grinned.

– You look offended. Like a good Catholic should.

– I'm not a Left Footer. And is any of what you just said true?

– Of course. Read your history books.

She kisses her fingers, places these same fingers reverently on the feet of the Madonna and stands up.

– The Madonna. Venus. Diana. The pagans knew more than we do.

She gets up and walks out into the bright sunshine. He follows her out. They walk together for a while. Mark talks about Sue and about Anna. She just lets him talk.

– Is she still in a coma?

– No. She's awake now.

– You should take her a bunch of grapes.

– Well, her friend asked me to. I got a phone call from her as I was about to go into the church to get married.

– What did she say?

– She said Anna was awake and wanted to see me.

– You really had a great wedding day, didn't you? You wouldn't think it was possible to top getting married, but you managed it.

– It's wonderful you find my life amusing.

– Because it happened to you and not me.

– Well, I didn't go, obviously.

– Obviously?

– No, not obviously. I didn't go because . . . I don't know why I didn't go. I came here instead.

– That must be killing you.

He shrugs. He had felt nothing for so long during his marriage and now he feels everything at once.

– Don't underestimate having your heart broken.

– If you want to feel sorry for yourself, come and join me in the burns ward. There're some five year olds who know a bit more than you do about pain.

– I know the way that story goes. Be grateful for what you have, count your blessings. But if we all counted our lives fortunate because we weren't in a house fire when we were five, none of us would ever want anything more than a beanie and a cardboard box for someone to drop coins in.

– I didn't mean to belittle what you're feeling right now.

– No, of course you didn't. But like you said, it happened to me and not you. So it's easier to have perspective.

They walk on in silence. Heat ripples the black ribbon of the road. An endless plain, lonely and barren.

Ten

Paul comes every day, first thing in the morning and then late at night after work. Today he brings me bananas and dark chocolate. I eat the bananas and leave the chocolate. I wonder if he knows me as well as he should.

I can see how I like this man. I just can't imagine actually falling in love with him. In fact, I know nothing at all about me, except what they say. But they could be talking about a stranger. This doesn't feel like me at all. Because this is what I used to do, is this what I am?

My mother comes every day. She brings a different photograph album every day and I experience my life from the safety of Kodachrome.

This is me. A freckle faced kid. A gangly teenager. A beautiful and tanned woman leaning against a rail, a waterfall in the background. She was happy. They all agree on that.

And still memory eludes me.

Soon after my mother leaves, Sally bursts in.

Mark D'Arbanville

I have hidden the book she gave me in a bedside drawer. Now I take it out and set it on my lap.

– Sally, I have a question.

There, that look on her face again. She must know what I am about to ask. But she must have wanted me to know, otherwise why would she have put the photograph in the book?

– Who's this in the photograph? There's no caption.

– Anna, there's something you should –

And then Paul arrives, the first time he has ever arrived at the hospital early. He is holding a large bouquet of flowers. Red roses. They are beautiful. My heart fills.

Sally snatches back the book and puts it on her lap.

I see the guilty expression on her face, like a wife with a secret love letter. But whose secret is she keeping, hers or mine? There is something about the photograph and the way I am drawn to it. And Sally knows.

Paul tries to put the roses in a vase but he fumbles. The vase falls and the water spills on the carpet.

As I watch my husband and my best friend clean up the mess I feel a growing disquiet. I have inherited a wonderful life, haven't I?

Then why do I have secrets?

Eleven

Late at night, murmurs from the nurses' station, the clatter of an IV stand as a patient in a gown makes their way along the corridor to the toilet. I turn on the lamp beside my bed and open Sal's book to the last page where I found the photograph. But it is gone. I get out of bed and look on the floor. Has Sally taken it? She must have done. But why?

Who was that man smiling back at me in the photograph? Where is he now?

I go to sleep thinking about my mystery man. There is something beyond memory calling to me now. A tingling low in my belly when I think about that face.

I cannot sleep. And first thing next morning I call her.

– Sally. It's me.

There is silence on the end of the line. She knows straight away what I am about to ask.

– I was looking through the journal you gave me. And that photograph, the one I asked you about, it's gone. Did you take it?

Mark D'Arbanville

A long silence.

– Yes I did.

– But why?

– Not on the phone. I'll talk to you tonight, all right?

A sense of dread as I replace the receiver. What is so special about the photograph? What is so special about that man?

A long and unsettled day.

My neurologist comes to see me on his morning rounds. I feel something, something I cannot explain, something I do not feel when my husband is here. He reviews my charts, asks me how I am feeling, shines a light in my eyes, tests my reflexes, warmth, movement, sensation. I like his touch and it scares me. What am I saying, what am I thinking? What is wrong with me?

Perhaps it's the drugs they are giving me or the injury, what Dr Maddison keeps referring to as an insult to my brain. An insult. What does that mean?

I do not feel like the woman my family and my husband describe to me. I don't feel like they say I feel. The woman they describe seems to be a different Anna. Or was I the same Anna, and I felt this way then and none of them knew it?

What was I thinking? Who am I? What can't I remember about myself that is so damned important that Sally cannot tell me on the phone?

I think I can guess. And I am not so sure I really want to know.

Twelve

Sally is late. She arrives just as Paul is leaving, just a few minutes before visiting hours end.

She is not smiling, not the bubbly Sally I remember. She has a shoebox under her arm and she lays it on the bed.

– I'll come by first thing in the morning to pick it up. You mustn't let Paul find this.

– Why?

– You'll see, she says.

She leaves. I stare at the box as if it contains a ticking bomb.

In a way it does.

Thirteen

East of Astorga

He comes to sit in silence in a village church. For a man who believes in nothing it is a strange thing to do.

It is late evening and shadows lengthen across the flagged stone floor. He hears the door creak open and he knows it is Madeleine, sees her silhouetted against the light for a moment before the door closes once more. She walks straight backed and snake hipped along the aisle and they sit in silence staring at the large crucifix above the altar. It is illuminated by a single light that is angled upwards, from right to left. It throws the tormented Christ into sharp relief, highlights his tortured and agonised face with shadow and light.

– These Spanish Christs are so graphic, she says. They look like they come straight out of a Tarantino movie.

The Spanish church is a vision of blood and pain, nothing is sanitised. The Spanish religious artist pierces his God with nails and spears coated with anticoagulant so he bleeds and suffers the more, as the picadors do the bulls in the *corrida*.

– What are you doing in here? she asks him.

He has come to find a Madonna and pray for a friend but he does not tell her that.

– Just sitting.

She reaches for him in the darkness. She starts to massage his thigh, and even in the gloom he can see it in her eyes, what she intends.

– No, Mark says, but he does not move her hand.

– Are you afraid you'll be damned? I thought you didn't believe in it.

– I don't.

– I can be your Virgin and you can pray to the goddess and give me your offering.

Suddenly she straddles him. He puts his hand under the long flowing skirt. She is not wearing underwear and she is wet already. She grins, wicked and brave. She bites the lobe of his ear, very hard, to make him cry out, but he doesn't.

Her right hand unzips his shorts and she finds what she is looking for. And then she lowers herself onto him.

Over her shoulder he stares at the crucifix, suffering, bleeding, grotesque. The pinnacle of western spiritual aspirations. The image is repellent and he closes his eyes. A lifetime of indoctrination overwhelms him. A single iconoclastic act to confront the guilt and chains of his own past.

Still he thinks: I should not be doing this.

Is this what I believe in, is this what I hold sacred – duty, sacrifice, suffering, a religion that excludes women? Should I preserve it holy?

Mark D'Arbanville

Or do I believe in the Virgin, the goddess with esteem among her peers and among men, compassionate and tender but with sexuality and passions of her own? Which of these gods would have saved Susan? Which of them condemned her to die?

Oh God, Madeleine whispers.

Mark wonders what will happen if someone enters the church now. Will they tear them limb from limb like a medieval lynch mob?

Madeleine screws up her beautiful face in a silent scream. She comes so quickly and easily and Mark is in awe of her, for this ease with her own body has nothing to do with him.

– Don't, she whispers to him, not yet.

He is not even close. He is hypnotised by the image on the altar.

She puts her arms around him and holds him close. The heady mixture of blasphemy and desire has brought her to unbearable pitch. She comes again and her moan of release echoes through the ancient vaulted church.

He has never met a woman like her. She comes in rushes, like small wavelets on a beach, then suddenly a Pacific breaker smashes down unexpectedly and from nowhere. He puts a hand to her mouth to shush her and she bites down hard into the fleshy palm.

He sees shadows in the vestry. Someone has seen them. The door creaks shut again. Whoever it was has fled, discreet or outraged, or perhaps to fetch that lynch mob with pitchforks from the fields.

He listens to the ragged sound of Madeleine's breathing. Soon someone else will come.

Christ suffers still on his cross. It all seems so futile. Will he ever have suffered enough to make right all the pain in the world? Can't we hold spirit and joy and passion higher in our aspirations, as Madeleine says?

Only the Madonna looks kindly on them as they hold each other in the shadows. She smiles her innocent and beatific smile, ancient, from a time long before these Romans made a new religion from shame. He sees Her smile reflected in his lover's face.

She moves on top of him and as he comes he calls a woman's name, but it is not Madeleine's.

– What did you call me? she whispers.

There is nothing he can say. Their ragged breathing the only sound in the darkness.

She smoothes down her skirt and rushes out of the church.

She is wonderful. He wants to love her. Oh God, please let me love someone else and get Anna out of my heart.

The king of wishful thinking.

Mark D'Arbanville

Fourteen

My hands are shaking as I open the box. Packed inside are letters, cards with pictures of butterflies, photographs. What is this? There is a photograph of me standing on a bridge and on the back it reads:

To my darling Anna, Paris will be in my heart forever – Mark.

Suddenly she is sweating and her heart is racing. Who is Mark and why am I in Paris with him?

There is another photograph. New York. God, I was there with him as well.

Another note, an apology for an email. What email?

You don't have to be Einstein. I was having an affair. I piece together the evidence like a homicide detective. The photographs, the postcards. How I feel when my neurologist walks into the room. The crime and the victim and the chief suspect are all clear to me; I am an untrustworthy slut who sleeps around.

I put the lid on the box.

When Sally comes back first thing the next morning, I hand her the box. She takes it and opens it tentatively. Several of the postcards have been ripped, others are crumpled and torn.

– Anna . . .?

– Just tell me one thing.

– Oh God, Anna, I am so sorry.

– Did this Mark ever come to the hospital?

– He came once . . .

– Once? Just once? Did he ever call you after that? Did he ever try and find out how I was?

Sally shakes her head.

Anna turns her face to the wall.

– I don't want to see that box again. I want you to burn it.

Sally leaves silently, the box under her arm. I hear her sobbing as she gets into the lift by the nurses' station. Fuck, why should she care so much?

I bury my face in the pillow and weep for a woman I don't know, a woman I have betrayed, or who betrayed me. How can I ever know?

And I see a postcard lying on the floor, ripped and wrinkled from where I screwed it up tight in my fist the night before. I reach down, pick it up and flatten it out. It is a picture of a sunset and on the back it reads:

Penelope Cruz still 0/10. I love you – Mark.

I sit up and try to call Sally on the mobile. There is no answer so I send a text:

Please don't destroy the box just yet. I need some time.

Mark D'Arbanville

Fifteen

Villafranco del Bierzo

– Tell me more about this Anna.

– Why?

– I'm curious.

The heat of the day and they are resting in the ruins of a Templar castle. There are ghosts here, in the deep shadows under the broken walls, the ancient voices that murmur on the dry wind. Anna and that other life seem a very long way away.

– Anna's dead.

– You said she wasn't. You said she was badly injured but she was still alive.

– There wasn't one Anna. There were two. There was the Anna everyone knew about and the Anna that was a secret.

– How do you know about her secrets?

– She told me.

– Why?

– I don't know. Maybe because I was a part of the secret world.

She tamps some hash into the tobacco and licks the paper. She lights it and takes a draw, then hands it to him. The smoke is raw in the back of the throat, the rush from the hash only mild. He lies back on his pack.

– What secrets?

– If I told you, it wouldn't be a secret.

– Dump her and move on to someone else.

– Of course. That's what any sane and rational person would do.

– You don't have a choice.

The crackle of tobacco as she takes another draw on the cigarette and then hands it to him.

– She wants kids now. Of course. But I kept thinking, fuck, what a mess that's going to be. Hard enough raising kids when you have your shit together. I understood her panic. Biological clock ticking away on one side, time bomb on the other.

– What time bomb?

He does not answer, so she asks the question again.

– It doesn't matter.

He takes another long draw at the hashish and hands her back the cigarette.

– What about you? Mark asks her. Why did your marriage end?

He listens to a long and complicated story of lovers and husbands, none of them remembered with more than a sort of casual affection.

Mark D'Arbanville

– I'm a heartbreaker, she says, with something approaching appalled pride. It's what I do.

– Remind me never to fall in love with you.

– I'll do my best. But you know men. None of you pay attention.

There is a long silence. Just the rushing of the wind through the stone. The shadows grow longer, the hashish twists the clouds into different shapes and colours. Two pilgrims on a journey to further away from where they want to go.

Sixteen

I slip the postcard under my pillow.

Who was Mark? Who is Penelope Cruz?

Paul comes to visit later that night and I hold him and hug him with as much enthusiasm as he does me. I want to wake up to a perfect life. I am going to make my square pegs fit my round holes. I am going to be happy. I am determined about that.

– God I love you, Paul.

– I love you too, angel.

– I'm so sorry, for everything. I'll make it up to you.

He blinks, confused.

– Make it up to me?

– You must have been so worried.

I put my arms around his neck and hold him close.

– I love you so much.

What is wrong with me? He's a good man, a kind man, and he loves me completely. Just how badly did I hurt him? Does he know about this other man, Mark?

– Paul, have we ever been to Paris?

– Why? Do you remember something?

– I'm not sure.

– Paris . . . we talked about it. But we never got around to it. You travelled a lot for business, sweetheart. You went there on your own a few times.

I see how it is now. For my work. How was Mark a part of that? I think about this. And while I do Paul holds my hand and talks about what we will do when I get out of hospital, about how worried they have all been.

I cannot concentrate on what he is saying.

When he leaves I take out the creased and torn postcard and hold it under the bedside lamp to decipher the postmark. The nurse comes in and says I should get some rest, but I can't. They give me a sleeping pill but I hide it under my tongue and spit it out after the nurse has gone. I turn on the bedside lamp and stare at the postcard again.

Mark sits in the vacant chair next to the bed where Paul sat just half an hour before. He is smiling, as he is in the photograph. I want so badly to hate him but the bitterness and fury is slipping away, like wet rope, I can't hold it. But if I lose my grip on my lifeline, I will drown.

I feel again that passionate longing that I want to feel for my husband.

Who is he? Why did he love me?

And did I love him?

Seventeen

Cab Finisterre

Mark climbs down the rocks at the end of the world. The sea heaves and swells. He has with him a bottle of red wine. He drinks it as the sun rises in the sky then scribbles a prayer on a piece of paper. He folds it carefully and places it in the empty wine bottle. A message in a bottle to the gods, as the ancients did.

He thinks about Anna, awake from her coma almost a month now. She has no memory of anything, Sally had told him on the phone. It seems to him the wrong lover had the accident. He wished he were the one with no memory. If he could not remember anything perhaps he could be free. He would have a blank, fresh start.

Or would I? he wonders.

Because he had dreamed her before she came, a woman who would wake him, inspire him, teach him, be in tune with

Mark D'Arbanville

him, with that part of him he had kept hidden, as she had hidden so much of herself.

And she had appeared.

But even if he forgot everything, she would still be a part of him, so would he really be free?

The corollary to that was this: now that Anna had forgotten everything, would she be free also? Was she just her memories and her past?

Was she what she remembered of yesterday or what she felt today?

Was she the things she had collected along the way or what she drew to her now?

None of us ask ourselves these questions when we look in the mirror. But now she has to ask this of herself before she can start to live again.

Oscar Wilde once said that sorrow was God's holy ground. As Mark throws the bottle into the sea he says a prayer and hopes that happiness might be on the other side of his sorrow. One thing for sure, God was fucking with him again, a little amusement on an off day.

Where's a removalist's truck when you want one?

Eighteen

Finisterre; in Latin, *the end of the earth.* The town has the feeling of a beach resort in winter. The sky is an amorphous grey. Fishing boats, red and green, bob at anchor, and white caps fleck the sea beyond the harbour walls.

She is waiting for him at a café, a hole in the wall with a few rickety wooden tables and chairs. He hears the plaintive cry of gulls circling the stern of a fishing boat as it chugs past the breakwater. A waitress sits at the bar eating peanuts and staring at the TV, the Simpsons eerily dubbed into Spanish.

– I'm going home, Madeleine says.

– When will I see you again?

– You won't.

He stares at her. What is it that's hurt? His pride? His ego? Or will he really miss her?

– Why?

– I could fall in love with you, Mark, I don't think it would be that difficult. But I look in your eyes and I see someone else.

You try so hard to make it different, I know you do. But it doesn't work that way.

— That's crap. I fucking hate her. She just used me to put her marriage back together.

— You'd like to hate her, but you don't. I can see through you like a plate glass window.

— I don't want you to go. You're special to me, Maddy.

— Maybe, maybe not. But whatever the truth she's still there in your eyes and I can't compete.

— You're wrong, he tells her, but of course she is right.

— Goodbye, she says, and she walks out of his life.

Sort of.

Nineteen

Sally is standing there at the door, a smile in place. But there is apprehension in her eyes, a sapper about to defuse a bomb and wondering if the wiring is outside her experience.

– Hey, Anna, you look much better today.

– I look like crap.

– Buzz cuts are really trendy.

– If you're a man or a lesbian.

Sally sits down beside the bed. There is a long and difficult silence.

– Sal, they're sending me home.

– I know.

– I'm petrified. I know Paul is as well. He doesn't know who I am anymore. Did he . . . did he ever really understand me before?

Sally doesn't answer directly and I search her face for clues.

– You and Paul were great together but you can be a bit fiery and your personalities are so different. You're very passionate, Anna, and very creative . . .

Mark D'Arbanville

– And a slut?

Sally puts her hand on mine.

– Anna, what are you saying? It wasn't like that. You and Mark were . . . I don't know . . .

– What? Say it.

– You fed off each other all the time, you were like electricity to be around. You sparked off everything you both thought or felt, you both challenged each other to your limits. You were *special*.

– Wasn't it like that with Paul?

She shrugs.

– It was . . . very different.

I think about this.

– How did I meet him?

– Mark's a scriptwriter. You were a film producer. In a way, you were kind of made for each other.

– But I mean, how did it happen?

– I don't know. You never told me, not exactly. You were kind of a very private person.

A very private person. So private it seems hardly anyone knows who I really am. Even my best friend.

– I want to meet him, Sally. Can you arrange it?

– He's been away. In Europe.

– Is he back?

Even as the words come out of my mouth I feel as if I have just split in two, one half eager and excited, the other wanting to run away as fast and as far as I can. But I have to do this, I have to speak to him, have to know what role he has played in my life.

– I suppose I can find out.

– What? I ask, seeing her expression. There is something she is not telling me.

– Well. When you started to wake from the coma, I called him then.

– You called him?

– He asked me to. When he came here that one time. He asked me to let him know if you came out of the coma. I called him and said you wanted to see him.

– But I didn't. I didn't even remember him when I woke up.

Sally looks shamefaced.

– I know. I called four, five weeks ago when you first started to stir. I just thought . . .

She shrugs, unable or unwilling to say just what she thought.

– And what did he say?

– Maybe . . . I don't know, maybe he's moved on.

– So we couldn't have been that special?

Sally shrugs and goes to the door.

– Sally.

She stops and turns.

– Were there other affairs?

She shakes her head.

– Then why Mark?

– You're the only one who can answer that question, Anna. Maybe because he . . . because you were special, when you were together. That's why.

She looks very sad. It shocks me, her expression.

– I'll call him. I'll tell you what he says. Are you sure you want to?

Mark D'Arbanville

– I have to do this, Sally. I don't know why, I just have to.
Sally nods.
– I'll see what I can do, she says, and walks out.

Twenty

Paul ties a blindfold around my eyes. He takes my hand and leads me from the car. I am coming home.

When he takes off the blindfold I look around at the house where I have lived these last five years and there is not a thing that is familiar; a chintz sofa, a Regency fireplace, photographs in heavy silver frames. The house has been filled with roses. There are candles burning and Katie Melua playing softly on the stereo.

Over the fireplace there is a sign:

Welcome home sweetheart I have missed you.

– Oh God I love you, Paul, I murmur. I put my arms around his neck and hug him. What on earth was wrong with me? Why would I ever have wanted to sabotage all this?

There is chilled Moet on the table and he pours a flute of champagne for me.

– Where's yours, sweetheart?

– I don't drink.

Mark D'Arbanville

Ah. Something else to remember.

I wander around, as if in a museum, staring at the exhibits, the souvenirs, the photographs. This is all mine yet it is not. Paul points out the objects like a curator in a museum: a photograph taken with my sister at her wedding, one with Paul, our arms around each other's waist . . . He shows me his study with his computer and the poster of his football team on the wall: Heart of Midlothian.

I am relearning the history of my life, swatting up, thumbing through pages and remembering dates and events and important names. Is this what a life is? Then why do I feel so disconnected from it?

The drink goes quickly to my head. Snap out of it, Anna. I am pleased to discover myself laughing. This is my home.

This is my home!

And then we go up to the bedroom and I stare at the bed and then at Paul. He kisses me on the shoulder.

– Sweetheart, I . . .

– What was it like, Paul? Was it always good for you?

He looks a little shocked that I should ask.

– You know you can be honest. If I was crap tell me and we can start all over again.

Paul gives her a weak smile.

– It's great, Anna, it always has been, but you are away a lot and so am I, so it wasn't as frequent as before.

– Was I a virgin when you met me?

– Yes, of course.

I take off my clothes, strip naked in front of him.

– Then I can be a virgin again. Like the very first time.

– Oh God, Anna.

– Tell me what you like . . . what do you love, what do I do that really turns you on?

But he seems confused. He does not seem to know how to answer. It is clear to me that my questions have unnerved him.

– I just want to love you, sweetheart, he whispers. I love you so much.

He is a gentle and considerate lover, even though he must be desperate for love from me after so long. I want him inside me, to know that everything is going to be all right. I guide his penis into me, wrap my arms around him, tell him I love him and that it will all be okay, and in the silence it is done. I feel him give a shudder as he spends himself inside me.

His weight relaxes onto me, and from somewhere deep inside me I feel something break, the anger and despair and confusion spilling out of me. I roll away from him and curl on my side. I hear someone sobbing and gasping for breath and I realise it is me.

Paul holds me, gentles me, until the spasm has passed. He does not ask me about it, just lets it be.

Later we lie in bed and talk about the specialist's appointments. I still have to go to physiotherapy although the doctors have told me that my physical recovery is miraculous. I stumble sometimes when I walk but my motor responses are unaffected. There is also an appointment with a psychotherapist. My neurologist, apparently, thinks it will help. Paul is going to come with me.

Paul is concerned; he has a job now, and he is worried about taking more time off work. He has to drive to Glasgow later that week and hates the idea of leaving me alone.

Mark D'Arbanville

I nod and tell him I understand. I am secretly relieved. It will give me time to work out what I can do about this stranger, this interloper called Mark.

Twenty-one

He never knew Sally that well. Bad idea to get too involved with your lover's friends. He meets her in a coffee shop at Paddington station, their conversation difficult over the station announcements and the muted hum of the commuters around them.

She is ten minutes late.

– You got a tan, she says when she sees him.

– It's called pilgrim brown. My back's got a big white patch the shape of a backpack.

A long moment while he waits for her to settle, slip her briefcase under the plastic table, unbutton her coat.

– She wants to see you.

He drinks his coffee and doesn't say anything. He wants to see her too. Selfish. Stupid. He wonders if being without a memory is better for her. Then she can look forward, instead of always looking back. Looking back never seemed to have got her anywhere. Or him.

– Does she remember me?

Sally shakes her head.

– But you rang me that day and told me she wanted to see me.

– I know. I shouldn't have. I just wanted you to know she was still alive and . . . I knew you'd want to see her.

– How is she?

– There's this thing they call 'emerging' when they first wake up. She's only just started speaking again. She doesn't remember anything before the accident.

– Maybe that's good. They can tell her who she was with them and she can be that person and she can be happy. What about . . . is she okay besides that . . .?

– The doctors are calling it a miracle. She can talk and she was walking after just a couple of days. She still has to have physiotherapy.

– That's good then.

A long and drawn out silence.

– Is that it? Sally asks him. You won't see her?

– I don't know.

Not to see her again. The thought of not seeing her again leaves him feeling empty and cold. If she did not remember anything they had done, would it matter? Their connection did not rely on their history but that knowing he had felt the first time he met her, that same knowing she had felt too.

– She kept a box. In her office. Everything you ever sent her, the pictures of you together. It was like a little shrine in a locked cupboard.

He pushes a ham and cheese croissant around his plate. It has cooled to the consistency of rubber. His coffee is cold.

– And you showed it to her?

The Naked Heart

She nods. He was about to ask her why she had done that but if he heard Anna's best friend tell him that it was because there was something special about them, everything he had ever thought, he didn't think he could stand it. So he let it slide.

– Jesus, Sal. Do you think that was a good idea?

– It's done now. I even forced the lock.

– You know, it's not as simple as you think, Sal. She may be your best friend but there's a lot you don't know. She's the most private and guarded person I have ever met. There's a huge part of her that's a total stranger to her family and to her husband. And probably to you, too.

– We all show a different face to everyone, Mark.

– Maybe. But it's always seemed to me that what they didn't see was what inspires and moves her. That's not a face. That's a soul. But maybe I'm wrong.

A middle aged woman with peroxided hair rushes past them with Louis Vuitton bags; a man with a dog; a businessman in a suit reading *Sports Illustrated*. All rushing to get on with their appointed lives, busy with being busy, appointments to keep, appointments that will keep them occupied until the day the articulated truck or the beautiful woman taking our hand in the early hours of the morning stops them and makes them think.

– She loved you, Mark. If I hadn't shown her the box you and I would be the only ones who ever knew.

Sally watches him struggle with this. But she knows what he will say. They were never able to resist each other.

– I sometimes wonder what I would have done if she'd died that day, Mark says.

Mark D'Arbanville

– And what's the answer?

– The answer is, it wouldn't have made any difference. I'd still think about her every single day. And here you are, bringing a ghost back to life.

– You'll see her?

– What good is it going to do? What is it you want for her, Sal?

– I want her to be happy.

– Do you think I might still be the key to that?

– Maybe.

She watches him struggle with this.

– I love her, Sally. Yes, I want to see her again. I will always want to see her again, till the day I die. I'm crazy, I'm just fucking crazy.

He sees something in her face. What is it? In another place, another time, he might have thought it was envy. Perhaps it is both a blessing and a curse to love so passionately, and so much, and sometimes people go a lifetime and never do.

Twenty-two

I meet Sally at Coffee Republic on Gloucester Road. A grey November afternoon.

– Are you okay? Sally asks as I walk through the door.

I am shaken, and it shows.

– The taxi driver asked me where the coffee shop was and I didn't remember.

– Sit down. I've ordered us lattes.

– I thought it would be easier by now.

I wonder how I can tell even this woman who says she is my best friend the rest of it. I still have fantasies about the man in the photograph. I have slept with Paul just once, that first night.

What sort of woman was I before? My feelings seem so at odds with the picture everyone has painted for me.

– How are things with Paul?

– I have to ask him constantly where everything is around the house. The other night he asked me if I'd seen one of his

Mark D'Arbanville

socks and I screamed at him. How the hell would I know where his socks are when I don't even remember my own mother? I am going to see another specialist next week when he gets back, his mother has organised it.

Sally puts her spoon in her coffee and stirs endlessly and I wonder what she is thinking, how much she knows, how much she is not telling me.

– His mother told me we were planning a family.

– A family?

– Didn't I talk to you about it?

She shakes her head.

– God, you were my best friend!

– Why didn't Paul . . .?

– I don't know. I don't even want to have sex with him. I suppose he must think it's not the best time.

– I've found Mark, Sally says.

– Really?

– He's just got back from Europe. He's driving down to London to see you. I've arranged a meeting. Tomorrow, at two o'clock, here in Coffee Republic.

– Here? Tomorrow?

Sally nods.

No! This is too quick, I feel trapped and pressured. I need time.

– You said it's what you wanted.

– Does he know I don't remember anything?

– Yes. He knows.

– Did you tell him I . . .?

I stare at her. Her eyes are liquid. I don't know what to say to her. What should she tell him? She's right, this is what I said I wanted.

– Why are you doing this, Sal?

– He made you happy, Anna. He made you laugh. He was good for you. Maybe what you were doing was wrong, in some people's eyes, but he wasn't a bad man, and if he gets left behind . . . I don't want it to be because nobody told you. It has to be your choice.

– What did you think? I say, looking straight at her.

– I don't know. I never loved anyone that much. That sort of passion, it's scary, Anna. I was frightened and jealous all at once.

– What's he like?

Sally shakes her head and sips her coffee, leaving a fine skein of froth on her top lip.

– I guess you'll find out for yourself. Tomorrow.

Tomorrow. I guess I will.

Mark D'Arbanville

Twenty-three

I am alone in my house, staring at the wedding photograph on the wall. I wander the rooms like a ghost. There are scripts tossed everywhere around my study, posters on the wall of films I have made, letters and faxes from people I do not know.

I am told I was building a great reputation as a film producer. I have watched some of the films on video. They move something inside me, and somehow I always know how they will end. It amuses people when I tell them that.

But I don't remember my part in any of them.

The flowers Paul bought when I came home from the hospital are dying now. Dead petals collect at the base of the vases telling me it is time to move on. I pick up cards from people I do not know, wishing me well. The fragments of a life I no longer remember.

Who am I? Am I all these people, all these things?

Or am I the woman who gets excited when Doctor

Maddison walks into the room, the same woman who does not want to make love to my husband?

Is it me that is wrong – or is it my former life that was out of step with me?

What was that other Anna that is me grappling with?

I find hidden in a drawer of my desk something scribbled on a piece of paper and I recognise the handwriting as my own. I wonder when I wrote it:

Touch me again please, just one more time
Let the electricity run through
Drink me into your skin, your soul, your heart
Keep the words short just drink me in – can you do this?
I can, and I know you don't want this
But I need this, I am so thirsty for you
Just take me – explore me, use me, do what you will with me
*   just don't question me please*
Take my body and hold it close let your body work its way into
*   mine and move within the rhythm of our souls*
I want to take you on a journey, one that we have been on
*   before, can we do this?*
Can you do this?
Can you smell my skin and perfume and rise up and over the
*   pain?*
Can I make you gasp in ecstasy as well as pain?
Can I wrap my legs around your waist
Can I sit on top of you and smile – knowing you are inside
Can you stand me anymore?
Can you just drink me tonight?

Mark D'Arbanville

Is this who I was? If this is me, who does Paul and my family think I am?

I search through the drawers in my bedroom, put on a white lace top then one of jade green silk, a mint skirt, green army pants, a long black cocktail dress. There is champagne in the refrigerator and I pour a glass, then another, then three, put music on the stereo and start to dance, alone in my private world again, to my empty blue sky, George Michael, Freedom.

I stare at myself in the mirror, my face stained with mascara tears, drunk, dressed crazily in the black dress with the jade top creased underneath, the rest of my wardrobe scattered around the living room carpet. What must I look like to the world, hair still short like a boy, those wild and frightened blue eyes?

Who the fuck am I?

Whoever I am, I hate myself, hate this stranger I have woken to, this bitch, this lying fucking witch. And I hate the man in the photograph. He is a sleazy lying bastard and he colluded with this other woman in the mirror, dragged me into this and hurt Paul and turned me into a slut.

Then I dance again, laughing like a schoolgirl, spinning around and around, then giddy, I drop to my knees, and beat at the carpet with my fists. I want to die. Why didn't they let me die?

What happens if I never remember?

What happens if I do?

Twenty-four

I wake to the insistent ring of my mobile phone. I am lying on the bed, still wearing the black dress. I still have my make-up on and my eyes are stinging from the mascara. There is a glass flute next to the bed, rimmed with lip gloss, half full of warm champagne. God, I must have drunk the whole bottle last night.

I sit up. I think I am going to be sick. I pick up the phone, flip it open.

– Anna? It's Sally. I was just calling to say good luck today.

– Good luck?

– You're meeting with Mark.

– Today? No, please not today.

– But, Anna –

– No, Sally, call him and tell him I can't see him. I don't want to see him. Tell him anything. Tell him I'm dead. Not today, please.

– I can't Anna. I won't. He came all the way to London just to see you.

Mark D'Arbanville

Oh God. I can't do this.

– Can you come with me?

– Of course. Look, Anna, just talk to him. Then if you want you don't ever have to see him again.

I hang up the phone and go downstairs. The lounge room looks like there has been a party with a hundred people. There are CDs strewn everywhere, their cases thrown carelessly aside, clothes hanging over the backs of chairs, rumpled on the floor.

I shower and throw on anything I can find, the jade top, a black skirt. I examine my reflection in the mirror. If this Mark loved me once the sight of me today should make him change his mind.

Anyway, I don't want to look good. I don't want him to still love me. And yet . . . and yet there is another part of me that wants very much to be the woman he was with in Paris, the woman he loved so passionately.

I spend hours putting on make-up, trying on different tops and dresses, blow drying my hair a thousand different ways. How many ways can you style hair this short? At least so that it covers this scar, this reminder that someone has seen inside my head. I look ugly. Why bother?

But I do. Looking good for him is just going to be good for my confidence, that's all. I am of course not doing this for a photograph, for a lover I cannot remember, a man I hate for destroying a life I can no longer remember.

Twenty-five

– Anna. Anna, are you still not ready?

I hear Sally calling downstairs. She has been waiting almost half an hour, while I stand here in the bathroom staring at my reflection, at a face I don't know, that I am still growing to know, like a new friend, a new lover, a new baby.

If I stare at her long enough, I see so many other images and faces. Are they fragments of my past or of something else?

Sally walks into the room.

– Anna, I was calling you. Didn't you hear me?

I feel frozen.

– When you don't answer I get scared.

I know what is on her mind. She asked me once: did you drive in front of that truck on purpose? I cannot remember. And no one else will ever know the answer to that.

– Anna, it will be all right, I promise.

As we walk out to the car I feel the sunlight on my back and I stop and turn my face towards it. It is warm on my skin. It is just inside that I feel frozen.

Mark D'Arbanville

– I don't want to do this, Sally.

– You can't change your mind now.

– I have a hangover. I drank too much last night. Tell him I'll see him tomorrow.

– Anna, I love you, I do, but you always run away from things. It's time to meet them head on. You're going to talk to him if I have to drag you there by your hair. Which is growing back quite well, by the way.

– I look like crap.

– No, actually you piss me off. You are just a few days out of hospital and you look like a model off MTV. Whatever else you've forgotten, you haven't forgotten how to make yourself look good.

– You're right. I'm being pathetic and a bitch.

I get in the car.

As we drive I stare at the crowded London streets, the black Austin cabs and the London buses, the posters on their sides advertising the latest musical, an Abba revival. I feel gooseflesh on my skin.

– Did I like Abba?

– More than was good for you, Sally laughs.

– Finally meeting my Waterloo, I say, but this time Sally doesn't laugh. We both know this meeting with Mark might cause more problems than it solves, but now we're on our way I don't want to turn back. I feel nervous and eager.

I feel like a bitch. I feel like a goddess. I feel like me.

Twenty-six

He sits in the car and watches the two women walk arm in arm along the street. When he first sees her it is as if his heart has stopped. He cannot breathe.

Anna.

The last time he saw her she had a tube down her throat helping her to breathe, and half her head shaved. That day he walked away from the hospital and vowed he would stay out of her life, if she survived. They had said goodbye once and she had told him to move on, and he tried to forget her. He thought it best to leave her destiny to the family and friends who were part of her world. He was just a shameful secret.

God, he thought he should never see her again.

He hesitates as he gets out of the car. What about Paul? Perhaps he is a nice guy and a good man. But if he is, how did he let her wither from neglect for so long?

What am I doing here? he thinks.

I have to see her again.

Mark D'Arbanville

Twenty-seven

We stop outside the coffee shop. My knees are literally shaking.

— Sally . . . I should do this myself.

— Whatever you want, Anna.

— Come back in half an hour. I'm sorry, after begging you to come with me.

— I can do some shopping. Here's that photograph again, in case . . .

— In case I don't recognise him? In case he doesn't recognise me?

— I guess.

— Thank you, Sally.

I feel as if I am going to be sick. I take a deep breath.

And suddenly he is beside me, holding open the door.

— Hello, Anna. And he smiles. He has deep blue eyes and the most wonderful smile. This is wrong. I am wrong.

I fumble my bag and all the contents fall on the footpath.

He stoops to help me pick up my purse, my credit cards, make-up – fuck, a tampon! I feel clumsy, crazy.

– You look incredible.

– I look like shit.

– You haven't changed a bit, he says, grinning. They tell me you've forgotten everything except how to be self deprecating.

– What are you talking about? What does that mean?

He shrugs and says nothing. I am aware of the scent of him, a warm male smell, *Miracle Pour Homme*. How do I know that? The memory of it nudges something inside me.

We go inside steamy warm after the cold outside and sit at one of the tables. I watch him order coffees at the counter, so calm and composed, and I hate him through to my boots. Why did he have to just appear like that and make me drop everything? Why is he the one ordering the coffees, taking charge? I dislike him instantly.

He comes back to the table with the coffees and sits down. And I want him to kiss me. I want to make love to him. Oh my God. His eyes are so intense and so blue . . . and wet. I could not have been more shocked if he had pulled out a gun and threatened to shoot me.

– What's wrong? I say.

– Fuck. This isn't going to work, he says, and stands up to leave.

– Where are you going?

– I promised myself I wouldn't let you affect me again. This was a mistake.

– Don't go, I hear myself say to him. Don't go, please.

Mark D'Arbanville

I don't know what makes me say that. But now we are here, I have to know what this man is like.

— I never thought I'd see you again.

— You hoped I'd die?

— To be honest I thought you would be too stubborn to live.

— Stubborn? Is that what I was . . . stubborn?

He sits down, looks out of the window, crosses and uncrosses his legs.

— You were the most stubborn and inflexible woman I've ever met in my whole life. Headstrong would be an understatement. Once you saw something one way you never changed your mind. It was a point of pride with you, of principle. You would cut your nose off to spite your face every single time. You were an absolute piece of work.

My God. This is the man who loved me? His first words are a damning analysis of all that is worst in my character.

— Why on earth did you love me then?

— Because you were also the most beautiful, passionate and creative woman I ever found or hoped to find in this world or the next. From the very first moment I felt like I'd known you my entire life. Every time I see you, you take my breath away. You are also impossibly contrary, bewildering and complicated. You are more high maintenance than a nuclear reactor.

— You don't love me, I murmur. You hate me.

— I have done both, lots of times. There's no one in my life who has made me so mad, and no one I have cared about as much either.

His eyes lock onto mine.

I will myself to remember something, but I can't. I am in a coffee shop a hundred yards from Gloucester Road station talking to a man I want desperately to touch, who has just told me he hates me, and who I do not remember at all.

And I want to tear off his clothes.

Mark D'Arbanville

Twenty-eight

– Why did you only come and see me once?

I do not give him time to respond.

– And you only called once. Is that how you show how much you cared about me?

– Well, you know. All these women I have in hospitals around the country. It's hard to keep up.

– What does that mean?

– You used to laugh at my jokes.

– I don't remember you at all, Mark. I don't know who you are or what you want from me or what we had. I don't know and I am not sure I want to. You're right. I think this was a mistake.

I stand up. He looks tired and desperate.

– Please. Just . . . finish your coffee at least.

My coffee: latte and very hot. How does he know that? I only just discovered this myself.

And suddenly I remember something, like a bright flash in

my head: a painting by Reubens. The neurologists told me that when the memories returned they would come this way, like subliminal flashes on a screen, sometimes images, sometimes sounds, sometimes smells.

— Reubens.

— What?

— Reubens. I just remembered seeing a painting by Reubens. How do I know it's a Reubens?

Mark shakes his head. There is a rueful smile on his face. He knows immediately what I am talking about.

— The National Gallery. We went there once. You were looking at the painting and I was looking at you. You caught me staring and asked me what I was doing. I said I was looking at a masterpiece.

A masterpiece! He means me.

Right now I feel more like a crayon scribble by a small child. But there it is, at least, one tiny scrap of memory, and it gives me hope that there may be a light to follow. I want to take this little treasure to Dr Maddison, like a star pupil with her teacher, showing him her painting, her essay. Look how clever I am.

— Anna.

Mark is staring at me.

— Sorry?

— It's all right. You were off in your own little world.

— Was I?

— You used to do that all the time.

Without thinking I take his hand in mine.

– Tell me, he asks. Do you have, like, a hundred boyfriends, or one really lucky one?

He smiles. It must be some private joke. I do not understand.

Twenty-nine

She is everything he remembered and yet she is not. They are the same, these small hands that touched his that first night, the long pale neck his lips brushed in bed and in other intimate moments a hundred times, and her hips, he knows the shape of her hips so well he can hold out his hands in front of himself and she is there.

Yet now she is a stranger. The memories of all they were are gone for her now.

Hers was a naked heart protected by razor wire. For reasons of her own no one had ever been let inside. Now here she is, his lover, the woman with whom he has shared so much ecstasy and pain, the best and worst of times, and she cannot remember him at all.

A stranger, and yet she is not. For he felt that she knew him at once, as she did the first time, as he did her.

– How did we meet? she asks him. Was it just chance?

– I picked you up in a bar.

She stares at him. Poor Anna, he thinks. She actually believes it might be true.

— You were wearing this short leather skirt. It's the first thing I noticed. Your underwear was showing. At least I think that was you. I have a lot of mistresses. It's hard to remember exactly which one was you.

He smiles. And to his relief, finally, so does she.

— The truth? We were at a screenwriters' conference. You waited up for me after everyone else went to bed. We talked.

— Did we sleep together?

— No, not straight away. You came up to my room. We kissed. That was it. You are the most amazing . . . well, kisser. In case you don't remember and no one else thinks to tell you.

— And the affair?

— I pursued you. I pursued you to Paris and New York and all over the country. I wouldn't let you go. We were amazing. If I'd had to, I would've pursued you through the gates of hell and a hundred miles on.

She sips her coffee and speculates. She is wondering what it was like with me, he thinks. She wonders what secrets I know of her, what intimacies of her body I know that even she herself has not rediscovered. She looks at him like he is a doctor who has operated on her and seen terrible parts of her body that she never can.

— So what was I like? she asks me, and there is a cold anger in her voice. Did I cheat on my husband because you had a big dick and you were good in bed?

He is not prepared for this but he realises he should have been. She hates him sometimes, he thinks. But if she cannot remember how the affair began, she cannot possibly understand. He is not sure he should tell her why he did it, why he thinks she did. Not now.

– Well we were very good in bed together but I don't know that I have a particularly big dick.

The couple at the next table turn their heads.

– Anna, it wasn't about sex.

– Then what was it about?

– I was trying to get a script produced.

The joke falls flat. She is pale now and her eyes are wet.

– I want to know what the fuck I was doing with you.

– I don't know. I was married. I had a grown son. I lived at the other end of the country. If you just wanted an affair, I was a very bad choice.

– I have to know this!

He takes out his mobile phone and shows her a text he has saved:

You have woken me and stirred emotions and desires that I thought only happened in fairytales.

– That's what you were doing with me. You had been married twelve years by then. That was what you were doing with me.

She stares at the message without recognition. She checks the date. Three years ago.

– I don't understand.

– No, neither do I. I'm just a man, Anna. How would I know? Apparently I woke something in you. I used this as evidence to believe that after all those years with your husband, you wanted to be stirred. I know I stirred. I didn't even know I was doing it.

– I have no memory of anything before the accident. Can you possibly understand what that is like?

– I have too many memories. I guess I'm a little jealous if anything.

– Tell me why I was still with Paul when I had the accident.

– I think there's probably a reason, and it has to do with the past. But you always told me I analysed too much.

– The past?

She stares at him. The past is what she no longer has, which is why the present she has woken to makes no sense.

She looks as if she is fighting for breath. He has seen that look many times, when she was angry, bewildered, hurt.

– Why the past? she repeats.

But Mark shakes his head. He really doesn't know enough, and what he does know, he can't, or won't, say.

Thirty

We talk until I have finished my coffee and I say I have to go but I don't. He gets two more lattes and we talk some more. *Drink me. I need this, I am so thirsty for you. Just take me, explore me, use me, do what you will with me just don't question me please.*

– What are you thinking, Anna?

– I was thinking I might like one of those blueberry muffins. I am starving.

He starts to laugh.

– What?

– I was hoping for some deep, heartfelt emotion and all I get is – I'm hungry.

And then Sally walks in. Mark gets to his feet and embraces her. She was his link, I realise. If not for her, this would not have happened. I don't know how I feel about that now.

Sally sits down. I get up to make room for her and spill my coffee over him.

Mark D'Arbanville

– Jesus, Anna, you haven't changed, have you?

There is soy latte on the crotch of his jeans. He leaves to find the men's washroom.

I turn to Sally.

– What did he mean, *you haven't changed*? Was I always so clumsy?

She shakes her head.

– It's not that. It's just that a couple of times you did some things accidentally . . . that kind of hurt him physically . . .

– God, like what?

– Well, once you told me the two of you were fooling around, arm wrestling, and your hand slipped and you smacked him really hard . . . in the balls.

– How was that my fault?

– You were both naked and lying on his bed at the time.

– Oh.

Sally laughed.

– Another time you were massaging him and you used hand cream with menthol in it.

– That's bad?

– It depends what part you're massaging.

She is laughing. For me this is just too . . . intimate. Sally's voice and demeanour change. She takes my hand.

– Are you sorry you came?

I cannot answer. I don't know.

Thirty-one

I lie in bed, think about that afternoon in Coffee Republic.

Touch me again please, just one more time.

Can I wrap my legs around your waist.

Can I sit on top of you and smile – knowing you are inside.

I get up and wash my face in the bathroom. I do not look in the mirror. There are scratches on the insides of my thighs. How did they get there?

When I left the café Mark had said he wanted to see me again, that there was a cottage in the country where we used to go. It scares me that a part of me almost said yes. That I wanted to say yes so much.

That night in my dreams there are hands around my throat, suffocating me. I can't breathe. There are men's faces, hard and cold. I try to fight them off but there are too many.

I can't breathe!

I wake up screaming and sweating.

Mark D'Arbanville

I fetch a glass of water from the kitchen. I can smell my own sweat and I strip off my pyjamas and take a shower. I stay in there for half an hour, and when I come out I find a piece of paper and scribble down some words, without thinking. They just pour out of me.

The world becomes smaller their words stinging in your head
Their hands sometimes like a snake constricting your air
That feeling of dread when you must pretend you don't care
That look that you have let them all down once again
Protective hands around your shoulder
That panicked feeling they are just like all the others
Around in circles my feelings go
One day I may want you, the next I don't know
Come near me, leave me, don't talk to me, come to me, a dance
of disguise.
My feelings I sometimes hide, don't look at me with despair,
I am not a person that you need to repair.
Dance with me in the light when you can,
Leave me when the dark enters and your touch is too suffocat-
ing to bear,
Don't ask for more than what is now,
Don't tell me I can be more
Just accept me as I am, and perhaps we can dance again some
more.

I have no idea what it means.

There is something lurking behind the curtain, deep in my soul, and I am too afraid to look.

Thirty-two

I find the diary at the back of my closet, in an old cardboard packing box, the kind removalists use. Anna had kept her school sports trophies, apparently she was good at sport, especially running. She has a Literature degree from Leeds University and there are photographs of her, flat-chested and lanky in her school uniform; at her confirmation; playing with her sister in the back garden.

I rummage through the box and I find some old photographs of people I don't recognise and then a little diary with a little key lock which was snapped shut. It has a beautiful little ballerina on it. I try to open it but it is jammed and of course there is no key. I am intrigued. I find a screwdriver in Paul's tool kit and lever off the lock.

ANNA JARVIS is written across the top in red. From the date on the first page I estimate that this Anna is about ten years old. I flick through the pages and start to read.

The entries are all made in my childish scrawl, in four different colours, red, blue, green and yellow. Depending on my mood, perhaps.

My God.

Oh my God.

I slump down on the floor of the closet, so astounded by the few lines I have read that for once I do not care about the cobwebs and the daddy long legs.

Dear Guardian Angel. I hate it I hate everything here. I am going to run away. My best friend has left, her father took her away to some other place now I will never see her again, it isn't fair. I don't have a special friend anymore. I hate going to school now. I feel so alone I wish I was someone else.

Dear Guardian Angel. Things are a bit better, we have a new teacher called Mister Hicks and he is sooo nice, really great and he is going to make me an Olympic athlete! He even thinks I can be on TV, he is my new best friend, thank you for helping me!

Dear Guardian Angel. In trouble from mum and dad for staying back at training too long with new teacher. Mum is being strange, I don't know what the matter is, dad is in usual bad mood I'm trying to keep out of his way, Mum is telling us to be quiet so as not to disturb dad.

I feel the smile freeze on my face. The warm afternoon has turned chill.

Dear Guardian Angel. In trouble with Dad, he hit me again today, I can't even remember what for. I think I touched some of his things. I was just playing and I think I smashed something, well maybe I smashed it on purpose because he threw out my records because I left them on the floor. Mum couldn't rescue them in time before they were all smashed. I didn't mean to forget to pick them up now they are gone. I am running away to the side of the house again. I hate it here.

Dear Guardian Angel. Fell asleep in wardrobe cupboard, mum had nearly called the police as they were looking for me and I wasn't in my usual runaway spot at the side of the house. Got in trouble again . . .

That feeling of panic again. I can't breathe. I force myself to keep reading.

Dear Guardian Angel. Mum and dad are fighting more now well Dad is screaming apparently we don't have any money but Dad has a new shirt and Mum is now crying which made us all cry. Dad left I am not sure where he went but we were happy he was gone as the screaming stopped.

What was it that Mark had said? I asked him something, and right out of the blue he had said there was something in Anna's past she could not remember even before the accident. Was this what he meant?

Mark D'Arbanville

Dear Guardian Angel. In trouble, mum is at school, teacher thinks my writing is strange, I am so unhappy I think I am going to suffocate myself or something she says that maybe I see too much stuff at home. Mum looks like she is going to cry but she tells the teacher that the story is good and she doesn't know what the fuss is about and that all kids have good imaginations. I love my Mum.

Dear Guardian Angel. I hate my dad. He says that I took something of his and this time I didn't. He called me a liar and said I was always trouble. I slammed my door so hard it nearly broke, luckily he had stormed out of the house.

This seemed to go on for weeks and then this:

Dear Guardian Angel. Mum took us all away and dad didn't come it was a great holiday nobody fought and we had fun. I don't want to go back home . . .

I cannot read any more.

I stare at the little diary in disbelief. Is this the same happy family that surrounded my bed in the hospital? It sounds more like a war zone, nothing like the picture I have of them all together around my bed. Did my father hit my sister as well, did he hit my Mum? Was I the only one?

Or has this Anna, the storyteller, made this up too?

I flick through to the very last page which is not written in coloured pen but in black Texta:

Dear Guardian Angel. I hate him SO MUCH he has left me and I don't know where to find him. Nobody cares, nobody would ever believe me, it would make Mum cry, and Dad does that enough, plus he would say I made it up they all would. Maybe I did, maybe I just imagined it. It is just one of my stories – angel yes I know that is what it is he wasn't real. None of it was real, none of it ever happened. Goodbye angel, no more stories from me no more diary no more you – none of this happened and tomorrow it is going to be okay.

Mark D'Arbanville

Thirty-three

I decide to clean the house and make something for dinner. Paul gets back tonight and I want to do something special for him. Something special for him to make up for seeing Mark. Even though he doesn't know about it. Especially because he doesn't know about it.

I plan the menu: asparagus in olive oil with grated fresh parmesan and scaloppine in a white wine sauce to follow, his favourite. He told me that once I knew the recipe from memory; now, as I prepare the meal, I have the cookbook open in front of me.

I open a bottle of wine for the sauce and as the bottle is already open I pour a glass for myself. I feel antsy. I shouldn't have gone to see Mark. What kind of woman does that make me? What kind of woman asks her best friend to set up coffee appointments with her former lover?

By the time the food is prepared the bottle is almost empty. I must have used more for the cooking than I thought.

I hear a key in the door. It is Paul.

— Mark!

— Hi, sweetheart.

Fuck, Anna thinks, and stops at the doorway to the kitchen. What did I just call him? I don't think he heard. What is wrong with me?

— Paul, sweetheart, I'm so glad you're home. I missed you.

As he walks through the door I rush to greet him. He takes a step back, surprised. I wrap my arms around his neck and my legs around his waist. I kiss him hard on the mouth.

— Anna, he says, but I have knocked him off balance and we fall backwards onto the hallway carpet. He is laughing. I laugh too.

— Hello, lover, I whisper.

I start to unbutton his shirt and unzip his pants. At least I remember how to do this. Didn't Mark say that this was what I was good at?

— Paul, I am so glad you are home. I have missed you.

— Oh God, honey.

— Is this okay?

— It's fine, don't stop.

Maybe it's the wine. My head is spinning. I roll off him, reach under my skirt and pull off my g-string. Paul's mouth is on mine and his hand is under my skirt and it feels so good.

I can smell him. But it's not Paul I can smell, it's Mark. Paul is on top of me, his pants around his knees, he still has his tie on and his shirt unbuttoned. I reach down between my legs to guide his penis inside me and I wonder if it was like this with Mark, how I touched him, how he felt in my hands, if it was different.

Mark D'Arbanville

As Paul enters me a part of me retreats with Mark. I can smell *Miracle Pour Homme*, it's on my skin and perhaps in my soul.

Paul comes, it has been so long and he cannot stop himself. I roll him on his back and straddle him, moving faster and faster. He slips out of me so I rub myself along his thigh. I close my eyes and there is a jumble of images and smells and voices in my head and as I come I am not sure who I have made love to there on the floor, but I suppose it doesn't really matter as I don't really know either of the men in my life.

Thirty-four

– **Thank you for dinner, Paul says.**

I sip my wine. Getting drunk twice in the same night. My God.

– I love you, I murmur, and touch his hand.

He tells me everything is going to be fine.

– I thought we could go to Paris for Christmas. What do you think? Like you've always wanted . . .

He talks about the plans but I am only half listening. My mind has taken me somewhere else, a smoky jazz club, men drinking beer from bottles, women in tight sheath skirts, the smell of sex.

– Anna. Anna?

– Sorry?

– What were you thinking about?

– Paris would be great but what about going somewhere where I can lie on the beach. The Bahamas?

He squeezes my hand.

– Okay, I'll go to the travel agent tomorrow. To tell you the

Mark D'Arbanville

truth, I think I'd prefer that. You were always the one that wanted to go to Paris and I'm not a fan of the French.

– What about Reubens?

– Reubens?

– Are you a fan of Reubens?

– Why?

He stares at me.

– I don't know . . . I just remembered something today.

– You did? That's great. What was it? What did you remember?

He squeezes my hand so hard it hurts. It's as though he thinks if he squeezes hard enough, he can make me remember more.

That night I lie in bed next to him, his head resting on my breast. I trace the lines of his face. He looks so peaceful. I feel a surge of affection. Paul. My husband. How could I ever have loved anyone else?

Suddenly a chill rushes through me, like poison through my veins, a cold mercury flooding through my whole body. What if he had been having an affair as well? What if I had been having an affair because he was? What if his love for me now is just guilt?

I feel cold, so very, very cold.

I jump out of bed and find his trousers, still lying there on the hallway carpet where he left them after we made love. Credit cards, money, tax receipts. I unlock his briefcase and start throwing everything on the floor. I find his wallet and spread out the business cards and there is a scrap of paper with a name and mobile number: Janine.

I find his mobile. She is there on the speed dial. I open the saved messages inbox. I am hyperventilating when Paul stumbles out of the bedroom, half asleep.

– Anna, what are you doing?

– What does it look like I'm fucking doing?

– I don't know. What's the matter? Calm down.

– Don't you fucking touch me! You have been with her, haven't you?

– With who?

– Janine, this Janine woman . . .

I hold out the mobile phone.

– The woman you have on your speed dial! How long have you been cheating on me, Paul – how long?

– Stop shouting, the whole street can hear you.

He tries to take me in his arms and I hit him on the chest, and around the face. He ducks his head and tries to grab my wrists and that makes me scream even harder.

– Don't touch me!

– Anna, stop it. Janine's my sister, she's my fucking sister, what are you doing?

I stare at him. He drops to his knees and he is crying too.

– I'm not the one that has affairs. Anna, I love you and I will love you until the day I die. You are everything to me – I don't need anyone else.

I curl up next to him on the carpet. What have I done? Who is this crazy, crazy woman?

– Paul, I sob over and over, I'm sorry, I'm so, so sorry.

He reaches for me and our arms and legs entwine on the floor.

Mark D'Arbanville

– Anna, you are my soul mate, you are the only one who understands me, the only one who believes in me. I breathe because of you, you complete my soul, you are the piece that makes it all work for me. Please remember me, please remember loving me.

My tears are so hot they scald my eyes.

I will myself to silence. I feel like I will choke.

Thirty-five

– You look like shit.

– Thanks, Jen.

– How was Spain? Did you find God?

– He wasn't home.

– Just as well. You probably wouldn't have got on. You both like your own way too much.

– You want some pecan pie?

– No, I'm on a diet. I'll have the double chocolate fudge cake instead.

– Healthy choice. I'll join you.

He orders the coffees and sugar overloads and sits down. Jen looks at him like he has a skin disease.

She has written scripts with him for years. Sometimes he shares her coffee and her office, at the back of her house. Since his separation from his wife she has taken on the role of script doctor and head doctor.

– I missed you, Jen.

– You've seen her again, haven't you?

– Briefly.

– You fucking idiot. I don't know why I waste my time. How is Sleeping Beauty? No, don't tell me. You saw her, she fucked you, made you crazy again, told you that you were the most special man in the world and then went back to her husband. You're in love with a pathological liar, Mark.

– She has no memory, Jen.

– Fuck, she *is* good. Better than I gave her credit for. It's the perfect cover. She can't remember a single thing she said or promised or hinted at, she's guilt free. She's a real peach, isn't she?

– She is not making it up, Jen.

– Fuck's sake, when are you going to learn? She should get an Oscar. Best unsupportive actress.

– She has a severe head trauma.

– How could they tell?

Even for Jen that was bitter. He wishes he hadn't come. He doesn't need this.

– Let's face it, would you want to sort this out? Two men fighting over you, lucky bitch, and trying to keep a lid on it. You wouldn't want it all out in the open, actually have to tell people the truth. Tell people the truth! Where will it end? If suicide doesn't do it for you, amnesia's a good second choice.

– I didn't come here for this.

– I'm sorry, Mark, but I can't stand it anymore. I see what she does to you. It's hard not to be cynical.

The coffees arrive. They both look at the chocolate cake.

– You can have my cake, he says.
– And eat it too? Then I'd be her.
He gets to his feet and walks out.

Mark D'Arbanville

Thirty-six

I smell toast and coffee brewing in the kitchen. I slide out of bed and go barefoot down the stairs. I feel Paul's semen sticky between my thighs and I remember last night. Paul is in the kitchen reading the *Telegraph*.

He looks wonderful, calm, reassuring. Everything has been forgotten.

– I am so sorry, Paul. About last night . . .

– Anna, let's leave it, okay? It's over, and you have been through so much.

– So have you.

I straddle him on the chair and kiss him, breathing him in. My husband. I feel my clitoris rubbing against the material of his trouser pants.

– What are you doing today? he asks.

– I am going to visit Cathy.

Cathy. My older sister has taken second place to Sally after I woke from the coma. I wonder why; it had been an instinctive choice to spend so much time with Sally instead. As if she knew more than Cathy ever did, or could.

    – Were Cathy and I close?

    – Yes. Very close. She was the closest friend you had.

    – She's taking me out to lunch.

    – Okay. Don't drink too much.

He is staring at the champagne and wine bottles lined up next to the bin. I pull his face towards me.

    – Honey, I promise. Look, that wine bottle from yesterday? I didn't drink it, I spilled it on the bench while I was cooking. Don't worry.

It is a lie. I watch myself lie and wonder at how easily it comes to me. Perhaps that was how I had been able to get by before.

Paul seems intense and uncomfortable now, and I don't want another fight. The mood between us has changed, and so suddenly.

    – Don't forget the appointment with the specialist tonight.

    – I won't forget. Unless the amnesia kicks in again!

He gets up to go to work.

He isn't laughing.

Thirty-seven

— Hey, sis. **You look terrific. Ready to go?**

I hug her. She is just two years older than me, and she has been there through my whole life. She knows so much about me, about my history, and I feel naked in front of her.

— Love your top, she says. Is it new?

— I bought it yesterday. I walked past this boutique on the way back from the supermarket. It was very expensive but I couldn't help myself. I didn't have anything else to wear.

— Anna, you have a whole wardrobe of beautiful clothes.

— Yes, but this is the only thing that feels like mine. Those other clothes . . . they feel like someone else's.

I can see the worry and pain in her eyes. We are so close, Paul said. Why doesn't it feel like that now?

It is a small Italian restaurant, Il Falconieri, not far from Gloucester Road. The waiter asks us if we would like drinks.

I pick up the wine list.

— Just some sparkling mineral water, please, Cathy answers.

– I wouldn't mind a glass of wine . . .

I can see by the look on Cathy's face that someone has been speaking to her. Paul! Suddenly I feel like a child. I call the waiter back.

– A bottle of Moet, please. We're celebrating.

– Your birthday? the waiter asks me.

– Just happy to be alive.

He looks puzzled but smiles and moves away.

– Anna, do you really think you should? You're seeing the specialist tonight.

– Did I drink . . . before the accident?

– Yes.

– Too much?

She shrugs.

– You knew how to have a good time.

– Well then, I'm just picking up where I left off.

– Just don't let Paul find out, okay?

– He shouldn't have given you rules for me. I'm not a child.

– He loves you, Anna, you have no idea how he was when you were in a coma. How any of us were.

She stops, and swallows hard. She fumbles in her purse for a Kleenex.

– We were all so scared that we were going to lose you.

The champagne arrives and breaks the tension. Cathy puts on a smile, and holds out her glass.

– To being alive, I say.

The champagne is very cold, sharp and acid. A celebration. But why, suddenly, did being alive feel like such a burden?

One glass is drunk, perhaps too quickly. Then a second.

Mark D'Arbanville

Cathy tries to distract me, but by now I am on my third glass and Cathy has just sipped a little of her first.

– I need to talk to you about Mark, I say, halfway through the antipasto.

Cathy drops her fork. There is a dizzying silence.

– Who's Mark?

– You know about him. Sally told me you did. I saw him yesterday.

Cathy throws down her napkin, knocking over her glass. The rest of her champagne spills across the table cloth.

– Stop, Anna, just stop! Stop it! You can't do this again, you can't do this to yourself or to Paul!

Everyone in the restaurant is staring at us.

Cathy lowers her voice.

– He's not good for you, Anna. He's not good for you in any way.

– Why don't you like him?

She avoids the question.

– He is totally obsessed with you. He'll destroy your marriage and your entire life if you let him! And after what happened to his wife, how could you even consider it?

– His wife?

– Maybe your friend Sally can explain. She's the one who brought him back into your life.

– I want you to tell me.

The waiter is fussing around us, cleaning up the spilled champagne. We wait until he has gone. By then Cathy is very calm, almost cold.

– Anna, his wife committed suicide.

– Because of me? Because of our affair?
She shrugs her shoulders.
– I don't think so, she answers finally.
But why does she take so long to respond?

Thirty-eight

We drive home in silence. The thought keeps tumbling around in my head: *I didn't die, but I did kill someone.*

There are shadows running alongside the car, dark angels. Apart from being crazy and an adulteress I am a murderess into the bargain. Why would any God want to bring me back from the dead unless he just wants me here to suffer?

I stumble into the house and collapse on the sofa, close my eyes, try to block it all out. I wish I was still in the coma. Fuck, I have drunk too much champagne. Is that why the room is spinning?

I just want to sleep.

Thirty-nine

I wake up at five o'clock.

I am supposed to be at the specialist's office in Mayfair at five thirty. Paul is going to smell the alcohol on my breath.

I rush upstairs and brush my teeth, find some mints to chew on the way there. I drown myself in Lancôme Tresor and phone for a cab.

When I enter the reception area fifteen minutes later Paul is standing there waiting and I know by the look on his face that he knows.

– You're late.

– Sorry. Traffic.

I try to kiss him but he moves his face so I kiss his cheek instead.

– You've been drinking.

– Yes, look, I'm sorry, I promise it's the last time. Please, please don't be angry.

He takes my hand.

Mark D'Arbanville

— If we want to have a baby you still can't be drinking, okay?

A baby.

The receptionist looks up at us.

— You can go in now, she says and smiles.

The psychiatrist is a handsome woman in her middle forties with a severe haircut and a tight smile. Immediately there is something about her I don't like. The way she smiles at Paul is a little too warm. I feel like a specimen. The crazy woman here to be fixed.

I don't think this is going to go well.

Forty

Her name is Dr Stein.

Paul and I sit on a burgundy Chesterfield side by side and Dr Stein takes a file from her rosewood desk and settles into a leather armchair. She puts on a pair of spectacles and picks up a Parker fountain pen from the green desk blotter.

I stare at the carpet. Pale cream. I am not ready for this, not today. Dr Stein is talking and Paul is captivated. I look up, and there is a butterfly at the window, jade and gold. It makes me smile.

– Anna.

I look back guiltily, like a child in class caught not paying attention to the teacher. I feel myself blush.

– Anna, you were thinking of something else?

– I'm sorry.

– If you can't concentrate there really is no point in you being here. Have you been drinking?

From the corner of my eye I see Paul's disapproving stare.

Mark D'Arbanville

– It was just –

She doesn't allow me to finish. Aren't doctors supposed to listen?

– Some alcohol now and then can be therapeutic, it can be part of the process, so you shouldn't be too hard on yourself. It only becomes a problem if you overdo it, when you are not clear enough to remember anything. You are just recovering from a terrible trauma to the brain. This is not good for you.

At least she didn't think I was an alcoholic. Or was I?

But I needed that champagne. My God. Was it a problem? How much did I used to drink before? Paul squeezes my hand.

– From the notes I see your neurologist is hoping some psychotherapy may aid your recovery. Do you think so, Anna?

– I don't know.

– How are things progressing for you?

– Some memories have come back. A painting. A jazz bar. She looks at Paul.

– Do you know what she's referring to?

Paul shakes his head.

– What was the painting?

– It was by Reubens.

– What was the name of it?

– I don't know. It was a portrait. A woman looking out to sea.

– Where did you see it?

– I did some research, I tell her, another bald lie. It's in the National Gallery. I must have gone there on my own one day.

– And the jazz club?

– I have no idea.

– This is unusual. Memories lost to retrograde amnesia do not usually return. Paul. How do you feel Anna is progressing?

Paul seems to flinch.

– I don't know.

– It is usual for a patient to experience long term problems with memory, fatigue, anger, dizziness, that sort of thing. This may be short term or the effects may be permanent. You have to expect this.

He hesitates, then looks at me for the first time since we have walked into the room and the pain is naked in his eyes.

– My heart feels like it's going to break. I keep waiting for you to remember something of us. But just this . . . a painting and a jazz club, nothing to do with us or the things we have done together.

He looks back at Dr Stein.

– It's like that little piece of hope is always snatched away from me. Nothing we had together all those years exists for her right now. I love you desperately and yet you don't seem . . .

He stops. There are tears in his eyes and he turns his head so I will not see them and tries to blink them away.

– You said at the hospital that you remembered my hands, but that's not true, is it?

– No. No, it's not true.

There is a long and aching silence.

– Anna, how do you feel about what Paul has just said?

– Sad.

– Anything else?

– Angry.

Mark D'Arbanville

– Angry?

– Of course I want to remember things about our life together, how we fell in love, but I can't force it! If it hurts to say what I remember and if it doesn't include Paul, I can never tell him anything, can I? I don't remember anything, all right! I never remember anything! Maybe I don't want to remember!

My skin feels like it is covered in cold grease. My heart is racing and there is a pain in my chest. The walls feel as if they are being pushed in, suffocating me. I have to get out, I have to find somewhere safe, but I can't move.

There is a dark light moving towards me and I feel sick.

When I come to, I hear Paul and the doctor talking over me. She is telling Paul that they will end the session now but perhaps he would like to bring me back next week. It is like I am not there, but I don't have the energy to open my eyes and tell her to fuck off.

Forty-one

Paul leans over the bed and kisses my forehead.

– Goodbye, honey. I have to go to work.

– What time is it?

– It's after nine.

– Why didn't you wake me?

– You need to rest. Doctor Stein was adamant about that. She said you had a long day yesterday.

This is medical jargon for *she needs to sleep off the booze*.

– Paul.

– Yes, honey?

– I love you. I want to have your baby.

He smiles like I have not seen him smile since the hospital. It feels good seeing him happy. Everything really is going to be all right. I have a home, a husband who loves me, good friends, a good family and soon I will have a baby to love.

After he leaves I step into the shower and let the water wash away all the dirt, the shame of the past and everything

I have been. Needles of hot water through my brain, my sins washing away. From today I am not going to drink anymore. I am going to get ready to have my baby. I will go to the pharmacy and buy some vitamins.

I put a towel around me and go downstairs to make a pot of coffee. There is a message on my phone.

From Mark.

Forty-two

Mum and Dad live in a terraced house in Walthamstow. It is much different to the plush address I now have in Chelsea. I am in their tiny kitchen. Dad is in a mood, ranting about something, and Mum is nodding her head but her eyes are far away. She has disconnected, just like I do. She appears to be listening to him drone on about something, but she is not really interested and he does not seem to notice or care.

Finally he goes out into the garden, and the door slams behind him.

My mother's eyes are kind; kind and the brightest blue, just like mine. They are kind but sad, always a little sad. She is sad when she looks at me now, sad for what has happened to me and sad too because she knows more about my life than she says.

She makes a cup of tea.

I can hear Dad cursing the lawnmower that will not start. Mum is watching him from the kitchen window.

Mark D'Arbanville

– What are you thinking about, Mum?

She bites her bottom lip.

– Just then when Dad was talking to you, where were you, where did you go?

She drops her eyes to the kitchen bench and I think she blinks away a tear but I can't be sure. She pours the tea. Her hands are shaking.

– I was thinking about an old friend of mine. We used to go to school together. I bumped into him at the shops with his wife.

I know somehow straight away that there is a lot more to this.

– Did you ever go out with him?

I have noticed she is a lot like me; if anyone ever asks her a question, she switches the conversation around so they find themselves talking about themselves or about someone else. But this time she doesn't do that. She sits down on the chair and her eyes go to that faraway place.

– That is why I told you when you were seeing that other man that you had to follow your heart . . . and that it was okay –

– What do you mean . . . the other man, Mum?

Fuck. She knew. She knew all along.

– I told you then, not to let anyone judge you, nobody, it was the mistake I made.

A long silence. She sips her tea but her hands are trembling and most of the tea spills into the saucer.

– My mother found out about me and Richard. That was his name. She told your father and there was a huge row and then I never saw him again. I did love your father. I mean, I do, but there was something else with Richard. Some sort of connection I wished I could have explored.

– How did you feel when you saw him?

– Richard? I felt like I was eighteen again . . .

– How was he?

There is a long moment of silence, a moment that goes for ever. Finally:

– He looked at me like he always did . . . like he could look straight into my heart.

I did not imagine the tears this time, they hang on her cheeks for a long time before plopping onto the formica tabletop.

Was I repeating the same pattern as my mother? Did she regret the choices she made? What makes you choose one person's love over another? I thought of Paul, then Mark,. and I wondered if Mark saw me again in thirty years would he still look at me like that? Would my heart still surge if I saw him?

I knew the answer, of course. I knew that it always would.

Mark D'Arbanville

Forty-three

He doesn't see me come into the bar. I stand at the door and watch him. He is nervous, fidgeting constantly with his drink coaster and mobile. But he has such presence. I can't take my eyes off him.

Can you smell my skin and perfume and rise up and over the pain? Can I make you gasp in ecstasy as well as pain?

He turns before I reach him.

– You're wearing Lancôme Tresor, he says.

– How did you know?

– I bought it for you. The first time we met you were wearing Chanel Allure.

I suppose he thinks he is being clever. I don't know really how to greet him so I kiss him quickly on the cheek and sit down on the bar stool he holds out for me.

– Vodka or champagne?

– Mineral water, please.

– My God. What happened? Are you waiting for a liver transplant?

– I'm not that bad. I'm cutting down for a while.

– And the shares at Moet et Chandon and Veuve Cliquot take a plunge. I sold mine when I heard you were in a coma. Mineral water it is.

– Your text said you wanted to see me.

His eyes are so intense, as if he can look right into my head.

– I had to stay on for a few more days on business. Thought I would show that I cared, he says, and gives me a wry smile. Some sort of barbed joke. Had any more flashes? he asks me.

– Did we ever go to a jazz club?

– Paris. La Huchette on the Rive Gauche.

– Was I there with you?

– Of course. Every man in the room wanted to dance with you.

I suppose part of me hopes that I wasn't with him, that perhaps it was Sally or a colleague from work. In my heart I had known it was him though, and a part of me, a big part, really wanted it to be him.

– This is so ironic.

– What?

– Your amnesia. You could never remember anything. We could have the most amazing and intimate moments and a day later it was as if they'd never happened. You were as easily distracted as a child. But now, when there's nothing else in your memory, you keep coming back to Reubens, and to Paris.

He takes a silver cigar case from his jacket pocket and lights a panatella.

– I saw Cathy yesterday.

– Ah.

His face goes cold.

– You know who she is?

– She knows who I am. You called her from your car once, asked her if she wanted to meet me. I still wonder how different things might have been if she had said yes.

– She told me what happened to your wife.

– I suppose I should have told you the other day. But . . . I thought maybe it was too soon. It's not something that ever falls easily into the conversation.

– It was suicide, wasn't it?

He nods.

It feels as if someone is sitting on my chest. I want to scream and cry all at once.

– I killed her, didn't I? Our affair killed her.

– No. We didn't. You didn't. Neither of us did.

– I murdered your wife!

My voice rises. Two public scenes in two days. If I had nothing to remember before the coma, I was making up for it now.

Mark grabs me by the arm and leads me outside into the street. Rain drips off the eaves; another cold, grey day in London. Taxis rush past in the street, the wet road hissing under their tyres.

He puts his face close to mine.

– Look, the other day, I didn't tell you about her because I just wanted . . . I don't know. It didn't seem kind. You just can't do this again. It wasn't your fault!

My tears taste of salt. His face is too close to mine.

And then I kiss him. I kiss him like the only way I can breathe is through him, and it goes on and on and on. Everything else fades away, the people staring out the window, the traffic hissing past just a few feet away. It is like I am a part of him.

Finally I break away.

– Why? Why did you do it, why did you destroy your marriage, your family, your life, for me?

– I didn't destroy anything for you. My marriage was already terminal.

– I must have been pretty good in bed.

A wry smile and he leans back against the wall. He looks desperate and sad.

– Wouldn't a prostitute have been cheaper?

– Yes, a high class hooker would have been a lot cheaper. Phone sex on a mobile with Cameron Diaz and the Queen of Denmark would have been cheaper if you add up all the air-fares and hotel bills.

– So what was it you wanted?

– Just you, Anna. I wanted you.

Mark D'Arbanville

Forty-four

She turns and runs away from him. He goes after her, the driving rain stinging his face. Her heel slips on the wet pavement and she almost goes down. He catches her by the sleeve and pushes her against a wall, under the eaves of the shopfront of an antique store. Rain splashes down from the gutter just behind his head. We must look like two crazy people, he thinks. We are two crazy people.

– It was me, Anna screams at him. I killed her!

– You didn't kill her!

– If we hadn't met . . . she would still be alive!

– It's not your fault! There were lots of reasons. I didn't blame you. No one did.

– Bullshit!

– You didn't kill my wife! You wanted me to go back to her! You kept telling me to go back! The only woman you ever tried to murder was you. That accident was no fucking accident. You pulled out in front of that truck deliberately!

She is suddenly eerily and icily calm. He watches a rain-drop track down and fall from the end of her nose.

– Did I love my husband?

– I'd rather you didn't ask me that.

– Did I?

– I don't know. You said you were the only one in the world who really understood him.

– What about you? Did I love you?

– Christ knows.

But she won't be put off. She asks him again.

– Did I love you, Mark?

– You told me I was the most special man in the world to you, when we were in the same room we couldn't keep our hands off each other, you said that when you were with me you felt free, that I made you feel like a sex goddess and the most beautiful woman in the world. Like I said, I don't know. Is that love?

He takes his cigar case from his pocket.

– You see what it says? *To my lover and best friend. Anna.*

– Did you love me?

– What do you think?

She seems to decide.

– Mark, I am having a baby with Paul. Please don't ever call me again.

And then she walks away and leaves him standing in the rain. It was the story of their affair. No two people ever said goodbye as well as Mark and Anna, for no other couple ever had as much practice.

Mark D'Arbanville

Forty-five

– Paul . . . wake up . . .

Paul is bleary from sleep. He sits up, pushing the hair from his eyes.

– Anna. What have you got there?

– Your breakfast, sir.

There is a rose picked from the garden, muesli, orange juice, toast, preserves. A plunger of fresh coffee.

– What time is it?

– Five am. I'm your early morning call.

– Honey, it's a bit early, isn't it?

– You have to be at the airport by seven thirty. You're flying to Dublin for work.

– That's next week, sweetheart.

I stare at him. Next week.

The walls close in again.

If I can't remember things Paul has told me just two days ago, how will I remember things that happened two years ago, two decades ago?

The Naked Heart   123

I throw the food against the wall. The coffee and juice leak down the plaster, the bowl smashes into pieces and there is milk and muesli all over the bedroom carpet.

Paul stares at me like I am a monster. Perhaps I am.

Mark D'Arbanville

Forty-six

Dr Maddison emerges from his office in a dark suit and bright yellow tie. Behind his smile there is concern.

– Anna. You're looking well.

He appears so assured, so confident. He ushers me into his office, asks me to sit, gets his secretary to bring coffee.

Oh God. I want him to hold me and tell me everything is going to be all right. Here is a man who doesn't expect anything from me, who just wants me to get better. He doesn't need me to remember anything about him. I can say whatever I want.

– How are you feeling?

– I feel like I'm going crazy.

– In what way?

– I can't remember *anything*.

He frowns and studies his case notes.

– You know, every patient is different, Anna. Some patients remember they went to a certain school, for example, and the dates they went there, but can't remember a single thing that happened while they were there. They will know their father was good to them but not remember anything they did together. Usually memory loss is worst for events just before the injury, events from long ago are more likely to be safe. You may not be able to remember your wedding, but it would be usual for a woman of your age to remember her school days, for example.

I just sit there and stare at him.

He consults his notes again.

– Doctor Stein has sent me a note here. She thinks there could be something else. An emotional cause as well as a physical one.

– I look at a picture of New York, I know where it is, I don't remember ever being there.

– Well, that is not unusual. What is unusual is that you have no memories at all before the accident. That's quite . . . rare. Have you had any memories at all?

– A Reubens painting. And a jazz club.

– How exotic.

He grins and I smile back. He holds my eyes. The moment is a little too intimate and I have to look away. He senses it too. He flushes and fumbles with the papers on his desk.

– Do you remember where these recollections took place?

– One was here in London, at the National Gallery. I think the club may have been in Paris.

– Do you remember anything else. If anyone was with you? Your husband, perhaps?

– No. I was alone, I think.

He frowns.

– And you think these memories are recent?

– I'm sure of it. I checked my passport. I was in Paris last year.

– That doesn't necessarily prove anything, but it is very intriguing.

I cannot think how to answer him. I wonder if he has sensed I am lying.

– You know, I wonder how things were for you before the accident. How was your marriage?

– It was fine.

– Fine. How do you know this?

– I asked my sister, my best friend. Why would you say something like that?

I resent his silence.

– My marriage was absolutely fine, terrific actually, everyone tells me that so I think you have completely the wrong idea of me.

– What do you mean, the wrong idea? Do you think it's wrong to have a bad marriage? Do you feel that reflects badly on you somehow? You seem very defensive about it. And how would you know? You can't remember.

I don't know what to say to him.

– You seem agitated.

– I threw my husband's breakfast at the wall.

A flicker of a smile, quickly extinguished.

– I'm wasting your time, I say, and jump to my feet. He is surprised and comes around the desk to stop me leaving.

– Anna, sit down. Please.

I feel like he can see right through me, through my clothes. My life is like a set of old clothes. I can't find them and even if I do they won't fit. And here I am, naked in front of everyone.

I run out of the door. Running again from feelings I cannot control. It feels to me like I have been running from these feelings all my life and I know it is time to stop.

I sit in a local park. I want a shower, what I feel is wrong, just all wrong, it is all my fault, making puppy eyes at him in the hospital and again now. What am I thinking? In a few minutes he travelled in my mind from being safe, a confidant I could tell my deepest secrets to, to being sexual and dangerous and someone I despised and who made me despise myself. And exciting.

I never want to see him again.

I never want to see Mark again.

But I knew I had to.

Mark D'Arbanville

Forty-seven

I had tidied the house, scrubbed the stain on the bedroom carpet and washed the wall. I threw out all the empty champagne bottles in the kitchen. A fresh start. My life would begin from this moment.

I find some photograph albums and start to flick through them. There is an edge of desperation to this. I am looking for anything to provoke a memory.

– Hi, sweetheart.

– Paul. My God, you're home early.

– Pack your bag!

– Why?

– I'm taking you away for a few days.

– Where?

– It's a surprise.

I feel a surge of love for him. This is just what I need. Beautiful darling Paul.

I run upstairs, as excited as a child, and throw clothes into a suitcase. I stop suddenly, hearing, imagining, a man's teasing laughter. The memory slips away like smoke before I can grasp it. I have forgotten about Maddison, forgotten about throwing the food at the wall that morning. I feel deliriously happy.

And then I hear Mark's voice: *You could never remember anything. You were as easily distracted as a child.*

My mobile beeps. A message in my inbox:

I have to see you. 2 pm tomorrow. Coffee Republic. It's important. I love you.

In a moment the excitement evaporates. I text back:

I am going away with Paul. I will call you when I get back. Sorry.

I wait for a response but there is none. I send it again, and again. Still nothing.

– Anna, hurry up, we'll miss the plane!

I stare at my phone.

– Are you all right?

I look up. Paul is standing there watching me. I nearly drop the phone.

– Yes, sweetheart. I'm nearly ready.

I throw the phone in my bag, a part of me aching. We catch a cab to the airport and he leads the way through the terminal to the British Airways check-in.

Paris.

We are going to Paris.

Mark D'Arbanville

Forty-eight

In the Louvre I stand in front of a portrait of a woman staring out to sea, lonely on a windswept Atlantic shore, waiting for a boat to return. But her sailor does not come. I weave a story around her, lost in the artist's world. There are always stories in my head, intricate narrative that comes from the blue sky in my heart.

I wonder about the artists who create such masterpieces of colour and pain. I wonder what inspired them, the private loves and agonies and ecstasies that moved them to create. There is ice in the Paris streets but I have warm coals again in my heart. Things will be all right now. They just have to be.

Paul calls to me, excited as a child. He has taken photos of everything, of the Notre Dame and the bridges and the Seine and the museums, he is fascinated by history and architecture, he is fascinated by objects and shapes and how they are perceived by the eye. He wants to explain the chiaroscuro effect achieved by an Italian painter. He sees lines and form and geometry.

I long to go to a bar and linger over a champagne.

Finally he relents and we find a bar. I drink my champagne, feeling wicked. He looks adorable with his glass of juice. I feel like a woman of the world now. I am okay. I am happy to be alive.

I am okay.

– Anna, I have to tell you something. It has been really eating at me but I don't want to wreck this time away.

Suddenly and violently I am snapped back to the real world, to crazy Anna and her problems.

– Before the accident . . . you hadn't agreed completely to a baby. We did talk about it but you were still not a hundred per cent sure and I just wanted you to know that . . . well, I can't lie to you, I have never been able to lie to you, you used to be able to see right through me . . .

Mark's face comes into my head. I feel guilty for Paul, guilty for Mark, guilty for an unborn, unconceived child. No, Paul never lied but I did, and I think he knew it.

Paul senses my mood and orders another champagne.

– Are you okay, sweetheart?

– I'm fine. Paul, I've decided. I do want to have a baby, I really do. One hundred per cent.

His face splits into a grin of absolute joy. It helps thaw my broken and disjointed heart. A baby would become the focus now, not me. This really is what I want.

But the nagging doubt persists, like a mosquito in a darkened room; is this really what I want? Why is he so desperate

Mark D'Arbanville

for this, why am I? Is it because I want to be a mother, or because I want to be able to focus on something other than what is wrong in my life and a past I cannot remember?

That afternoon while Paul is taking photographs of the artists by the Notre Dame, I wander into the Rive Gauche and find La Huchette. It is closed, of course, in the afternoon and I stand staring at the door and the posters in the window advertising that night's jazz band.

This was where I had come with Mark.

That night, shadows in a darkened room, I lie on top of Paul, rubbing myself along his thigh, alone with my private fantasies, sex alone and for two. I feel his semen sticky between my thighs. Soon this will be the residue of the baby we will make together. I am in Paris with my husband, I am the happiest woman in the world.

I am okay.

I am okay.

What more could I want? He is gentle, so gentle, through all my dramatic turns. Since the hospital he has never lost his temper, he forgets and forgives so quickly. He is never moody like me. He is intelligent – it is like having my own personal guide, this amazing memory for facts about politics and history.

He may know more about politics and history but here in the dark I am utterly in control. I arch my back as my orgasm starts its long and delicious arc through my body. In a smoky basement jazz club I am dancing hip to hip with Mark and I am whispering: *You have woken my body and my heart.*

Paul may know about the Renaissance and about

The Naked Heart

133

Haussmann and Baudelaire, but I am the only one with the power to make him feel, the only one with the keys to unlock his clumsy heart.

We lie there in the dark and I hold his head on my breast, and I feel safe. I wonder what had ever made that other Anna have an affair. Paul might be the teacher in the Louvre but here in bed I am his Michelangelo.

Soon we will have a baby together and everything will be fine.

I am okay.

Forty-nine

We get back early on Monday morning and Paul leaves straight away for work. He has to fly to Dublin and he will be away for two nights. I kiss him goodbye and collapse on the sofa and sleep.

I am dragged from a black and seamless sleep by my mobile.

– It's Mark. I need to see you.

– Where are you?

– My car's across the street. Put your coat on and come outside.

The roseate world of the weekend has vanished. I am back in my fractured reality, a Kafkaesque world I have created defined by intricate lies and painful deceptions.

I slip on my coat – I had slept in the clothes I had worn on the plane from Paris – and walk across the street. He is sitting behind the wheel of a maroon MG sedan. He leans across to open the passenger side door.

He looks terrible, as though he hasn't slept in days. It scares me. His cheeks are hollowed and there are dark shadows under his eyes.

He starts the engine.

– Where are we going?

– I'll tell you when we get there.

– Paul, where are we –?

– No, not Paul, fucking Mark. I'm Mark, remember? I know it must be hard to keep track these days.

– Stop it, you're scaring me.

– How was Paris?

– It was wonderful.

– Wonderful.

– I thought you'd be happy for me.

– You want me to be pleased for you that you went away for the weekend and slept with someone else? Why don't you just grab a garden trowel and castrate me with it? The woman I love more than anything in the world just went on holiday to Paris and slept with another man. Fantastic.

I am so terrified, I can't even hear what he is saying, I just know he is shouting at me. His whole face has changed. He hates me! He doesn't love me at all!

– Did you go to La Huchette?

– No.

– Did you remember anything about Paris? Do you remember dancing with me there?

– I don't remember. What's wrong with you? Why are you shouting?

– I used to wonder whether you showed him the things we

Mark D'Arbanville

did together, made sex with him better by showing him what we did . . .

His knuckles are white on the steering wheel. I have to get out of this car. I try to open the door but he has activated the central locking.

– Let me out!

– What hurts, what really fucking hurts, is that I gave you the keys to the castle. You learned what you had to do to get back in control of Paul. That's all you wanted from me. It's all it's ever been about for you! How to get control of Paul!

Christ. He is crazy. I feel trapped.

– Open the door now, OPEN THE FUCKING DOOR!

We stop at the lights at the end of the street and he snaps off the central locking. I get out and he takes off down the road. I hear a scream of brakes, he almost t-bars a cab at the intersection.

We have come full circle. He's the one that wants the coma now. He's the one who has to forget. Whatever that other Anna has done, I have forgotten and now he has a past that he can't let go of and can't forgive.

Fifty

I stand in the street watching until the brake lights disappear among the press of traffic on Fulham Road. My wrist hurts. I must have bruised it getting out of the car. Has he always been like this? Was he always so intense? So crazy?

Did he ever hurt me?

And then suddenly the memories are pouring back, but not Reubens portraits or jazz clubs, these are different, and I have to lean against a light pole. I cannot get my breath. The sky is falling down on me, and I am drowning, drowning in the air, there are faces, I cannot see them clearly, it is as if I am looking at them through water. I am going to die, there are hands all over my body, there is something in my mouth and I cannot breathe . . .

People stop in the street and a man asks me if I am all right and perhaps he touches my arm and I scream and back away as if he is holding a knife to me. A door is opening and I am falling into space.

Mark D'Arbanville

I have to get home. I have to get out of the street and home where I will be safe.

Fifty-one

I stretch my wings just slightly
I am scared that if I open them too much people will notice,
I want the spotlight and yet part of me hates it
The need to please
The need to not stand out and yet the conflict inside because
    I want to –
I want to make a difference
I want to be loved

I don't want people to hate me who don't even know me
I don't want to upset or disappoint and yet I do
I fly out into the open my wings stretched and I soar under the
    warmth of the sun as it sets
there is nobody around and I am at peace

I dance to a song inside my heart that nobody else can hear
    and for those moments I feel so light and my heart is free –
    no judgement

Mark D'Arbanville

no expectations
just me flying and dipping through the air the sun a beacon in
    my heart
The night is not frightening,
I am not thinking of the days to come
I just fly
for a moment clear and free.

Fifty-two

Mark walks the park, hating the small children, the cute dogs with their hand-knitted coats, even the fucking squirrels. She wants to be their good wife and good mother and good daughter, to be loved and to be popular, and not to hurt anyone and not to have bad thoughts. It seems to him she is trying to bang her round peg into their square hole.

He knows that as much as a part of her loves him, there is a part that hates him too. He had had the temerity to suggest that perhaps she had no place being in the marriage and the life she was in, that she was living someone else's life.

Perhaps she even hated him for knowing her secret. You can't tell anyone, she had said. And he didn't.

And now even she didn't know her own secrets anymore.

He has become crazy and angry and obsessed. The weight of too many secrets, too many lies.

142

Fifty-three

A card arrives by courier. On the front is a picture of a butterfly. Inside there is a handwritten note:

I am sorry.

I cannot stand this. I feel like I have been erased from your life. Everyone is closing in around you and I am being shut out yet again.

Forgive me if I scared you. I understand if you never want to see me again.

Always
Mark

Before I have even finished reading the card I am dialling his number. Strange, but I can always remember his number without difficulty. He asks me to come away with him that night to see the cottage where we used to meet.

I say yes.

Yes.

Fifty-four

My case with the British Airways tags stands awkwardly in the middle of the hallway like a guilty schoolgirl. I packed only new things. I have sent most of the clothes that were hanging in the ensuite to the charity store down the road. It felt as if I was putting on a dead woman's clothes.

A cab pulls up outside to take me to Gloucester Road station. I don't want Mark picking me up at my house. I am sick with nerves and guilt when I meet him, just as I was before. Perhaps it was always like this.

I get out of the cab and he is there to throw my case into the boot of his MG. I climb in beside him. He seems agitated behind the delicious smile. He looks so tired. I wonder if this is how he always looks or if it is just the strain of having me back in his life that drains the energy out of him.

– You look wonderful, he murmurs. You still take my breath away. You always did.

He is not the crazy man I met yesterday morning. As we

Mark D'Arbanville

drive towards Hyde Park I relax a little. I wonder what it was like with him before. Now when I meet him, I feel on edge, like he is going to suffocate me with his intensity.

But there is something else. Something that leaves me aching inside.

The drive takes us three hours and this time the talk is desultory. There is so much unspoken between us, and we skip around it as if it is an unexploded bomb. He talks a little about his work, about the woman he almost married, and about the *camino*. Paris is not mentioned, and neither is Paul.

And then we arrive at the cottage. It is ramshackle and the garden is overgrown with blackberry and there is moss on the roof. A horse grazes in the field beside it.

– Mark, it's beautiful.

– We came here a lot. This is where we worked on our script. When we weren't tearing each other's clothes off.

– We worked together?

He gives me a wry smile.

– You think sex was the only thing we had in common?

I walk into the cottage. I see on his face as I have seen it on so many other faces these last few weeks: the expectation that I would remember. It is beautiful inside, deliciously warm, someone has lit a fire in the grate, and there is a bay window that looks out over the chestnut trees and a pasture. But there is nothing familiar here.

Mark looks disappointed but tries to hide it from me.

– I am sorry, Mark. I don't remember anything.

– It really doesn't matter.

I sit down on the lounge. So beautiful, so peaceful.

– I had the caretaker put some champagne on ice.

I want some but I know what Paul would say. *Don't drink, Anna. Don't sleep with other men, Anna.*

– That would be great.

There is a single bedroom – I look in and move on quickly – and a study. There is a pinboard on one wall and Mark has pinned dozens of photographs on it. I see my own face in each one.

Suddenly he is standing behind me with the champagne.

– You remember this? he whispers.

I see myself grinning in the kitchen. I am wearing just a t-shirt – one of his – and holding a saucepan towards the camera.

– You'd just made chocolate sauce. You painted it on me and then you licked it off. Then I did the same to you. Then I . . .

– It's okay. You don't have to tell me any more.

I feel my cheeks burning and I cannot look at him. I feel his presence, the heat of him, even through my coat. It is strange to have been so intimate with another man and have no remembrance of it at all.

Finally I meet his eyes. The look on his face. I am thinking the same thing: I'm wet. My body has betrayed me again.

Who am I really? Am I this life I have inherited, or am I what I feel right now?

Mark D'Arbanville

Fifty-five

Mark watches her face, searching for clues. Why did she come? Does she feel obligated to me, or beneath all this guilt does she still feel that same reckless passion she once did, those same longings that tormented and finally nudged her foot off the brake and sent her careering in front of the removalist's truck?

The face she wears now he has seen many times, when she feels pressured or hurt or torn her face would go blank, not understanding what it was she was expected to say or do.

– This is Paris, he tells her. We stayed in Rue Chateaudun. That was taken by the Pont de Neuf. We kissed on the bridge. That night we went to La Huchette, the jazz club on the Rive Gauche.

She wants to skip Paris. All she remembers of it now, he guesses, is going there with another man. One way to exorcise the ghosts.

– Where was this?

There is a table set up on the sand, in the background the black silhouette of palm trees and a dipping orange sun. The distinctive orange label of a Veuve Cliquot bottle is visible in the foreground, protruding from an ice bucket. Anna looks radiant. She had forgotten about her world then; he had forgotten about his.

– The Caribbean. It was a restaurant called the Casa del Mar. I asked you to marry me.

– I knew you before I was married?

– No. But I asked you anyway. I was carried away with the mood.

– Were you always crazy?

– No. I got crazy after I met you. But I got to like me that way so I stuck with it. Crazy is good. Crazy is the only time I really feel alive.

She touches the top she is wearing, jade with lace trim. The same style as the one she is wearing in the photograph, only hers is new, bought in Paris. A part of her did remember. They both notice but neither wants to draw attention to it now.

– When you walked into a room every man turned his head. You never ever noticed.

– Was I a flirt?

– With me you were. But other men, you never caught their eye. I think maybe they were intimidated by you.

He takes out his mobile phone and shows her a text message he saved:

IT IS WINDY HERE 2DAY I HAVE ON MY MINT SKIRT AND IT KEEPS BLOWING UP. I SHOULD HAVE WORN UNDERWEAR.

Mark D'Arbanville

She blushes. This is not like her at all. Or is it? How does she know what she is like if others must tell her who she is? She passes back the phone without comment.

– This is Reims, he says. It was winter and you were running from one champagne house to another, you were a little . . .

– Drunk?

– Absolutely.

The champagne is going to Anna's head. Drunk again. There are so many photographs of this woman called Anna, so different from the Anna she was supposed to be in London.

– This is New York, she says. That's the Brooklyn Bridge in the background.

– It was taken at Southport. We'd just had a fight.

– We fought? What did we fight over?

– I wanted a life with you. You didn't.

– Why?

– You said you loved Paul more than you loved me.

– I said that?

– Then you said in the next breath that when you were with me you felt free and inspired. You understand why sometimes I got a little crazy?

Anna turns away and goes to the window. Too many photographs, too many memories she does not have. Who was this woman? What made her do the things she did?

There is a script on the desk. He nudges it towards her with his finger. It is flecked with blood.

– You don't remember this?

Anna stares at it, mystified.

– It's got blood on it, she says.

– It was in the back of your car when you had the accident. Sally found it and took it away with her before the tow truck arrived. There were some notes written in the margins and she didn't want anyone else to see them.

Anna is silent. He imagines she has no idea what to say.

– You said to me once that I woke you, sexually and emotionally. Not Paul, who you'd been living with for twelve years. Me, who you'd known not even a few months. Yet, if you could have made me disappear from that moment, from that very moment, I think you would have done. That's what drove me crazy. It seemed like you wanted things different as long as they stayed the same. Still. It was your life. But something must have jarred with you, or else you wouldn't have driven in front of that truck.

– Are you saying I didn't do anything that was good?

– I was like a blind man. You helped me see. Now I'm back in the dark. Is that good or bad? Jury's still out. Look, it's not your problem. Not your life. We all make our own choices.

He walks out onto the porch. He takes a cheroot from the cigar case she gave him and lights it. It is cold and he is just in his shirt sleeves.

She stands at the window watching him. She wishes they would all just go away and leave her alone, that she could start this new life on a fresh slate, away from Paul, away from Mark, away from everybody. Just be free.

Mark D'Arbanville

Fifty-six

I feel him behind me, his mouth on my neck. No. Fuck. Stop.

Yes. God, yes.

Don't.

Don't stop!

Yes!

I'm not ready to jump back into an affair that made me crazy before, when I couldn't work out what my life was like. My life with Paul seems so wonderful now. But if it is so wonderful then why am I here?

– I have missed you so much, he whispers.

His hands are moving over me and he turns me around. My head is spinning with the champagne, the photographs, everything, and I let him carry me into the bedroom, and back into the abyss.

A part of me wants to please him, ease his pain, give him back that part of me that he had before.

Is this so wrong?

Fifty-seven

I lie in the mess of tangled sheets. There is a wetness on the sheet under my thigh. His hand is on my inner thigh, his eyes are closed, and I can feel his breath on my cheek. His penis is curled along his belly. I feel a longing to stroke it and kiss it, and brush the thought guiltily aside. This is the part of me that I have to chase out of my life forever. So that I can be the woman they tell me I am.

Don't I?

I can't remember anything, I can't feel anything. I just feel numb.

– Hi, you, he murmurs, opening his eyes.

– Hi.

– Was I asleep for long?

He moves his hand to my breast.

My mobile rings. It is in my bag, which is lying on a chair in the living room. We both stare at it.

I jump out of bed and check the display. It's Paul.

– Hey baby, how are you going?

– Hello honey.

I see Mark's face. He knows straight away. I wrap a towel around me and wander outside onto the porch.

– I rang home. You weren't there.

– I took a drive into the country. I just wanted a few days out of London to think.

– Where are you?

– It's a little village called . . . I make up something in my head. Grafton, I think.

– Are you on your own?

– Yes.

There is dead silence on the other end of the line. Then he says:

– Honey, I love you. I love you with all my heart, okay?

– I love you too, baby.

– Look, I spoke to my mother today on the phone. She has an old school friend, he married an Italian woman, a specialist, she has a clinic in Italy. They are doing really good work on traumatic amnesia, with drugs and hypnotherapy. You remember your doctors and Doctor Stein thought that it might not just be the accident, there might be something else. I thought, well, we could go there if you wanted. She managed to get an appointment for you.

Silence.

– I know you think she's really controlling and interfering, Paul says, but it might be . . . a good thing.

Did I think that about his mother? I had no idea.

– Sweetheart, that's wonderful, thank her for me. We'll talk about it when you get home. Maybe this is what I need. I'll try anything.

The Naked Heart

– I'll be home tomorrow night. I miss you.

– I miss you too. I love you.

When I hang up Mark is right there behind me. He must have heard what I said. My breath catches in my throat. His face is unreadable.

– I'm sorry, Mark.

These two men, they are like polar opposites. If I could magically make the two of them into one person, I would.

He laughs when I tell him that.

– What's so funny?

– If you could magically make us one person you'd have *you*! Someone torn in two parts. Is that who you want? Then there'd be a foursome instead of a triangle! Putting me and him together? That's like saying you want a reckless conservative. It's a contradiction in terms.

– Maybe.

– Only one thing I can tell you from my own experience, Anna. A baby won't fix it.

– Don't tell me what to do, Mark.

– God forbid. He shrugs, looks suddenly more tired than I have ever seen him.

He goes back inside. I stare at my phone. Two men and one woman, a fractured woman torn in half and with nothing but a blank memory, and a life that does not seem to fit.

Mark D'Arbanville

Fifty-eight

When I come back inside, he has made the bed and is packing our bags. He points at my suitcase, my clothes just thrown in. Just the same Anna, he smiles as I walk in. Just chuck everything in.

– I thought we were going to stay here tonight, I say, and there is a part of me that is disappointed.

– I don't think that would be a good idea.

– It was just about sex, then?

– Because it's not. Because if I stay my heart's going to break again.

He takes a letter from his jacket pocket and hands it to me.

– What's this?

– It's something you sent me once.

I open it. I am nervous, it feels as if I am reading someone else's diary.

. . . I am a princess and I am being strapped into a ball gown that is so tight I can't breathe and yet I feel so sexy, so desirable, so alive, and I no longer care about the pain of the dress. I cannot wait for someone to slowly unravel me.

I am a call girl telling a man he is everything he wants to hear, making him want me, making him desire me. He wants to come in my hand, in my mouth, inside me, he will do anything to own me, have me, but still I tease him and watch his eyes blaze . . .

I am a mother with a young child running in the park. The child is innocent and beautiful and she needs me and loves me and I am so happy.

I am walking into a room of a thousand people. I have a brand new dress on, with a split right up to my thigh. I feel good. I drink some champagne, ignore the jealous stares of the other women, move through the room and flirt with every man whose eyes meet mine. Tonight I am perfect and I am happy.

I am at a party and I see her. She is beautiful and tall and blonde and full breasted. I want her, I know she wants me, her eyes take in every inch of me and as she moves closer she puts her hand on my hip and then it moves to my ass, and she is close enough that I can smell her perfume and all I want is to bury my face in her breasts and kiss her nipples and her belly and taste her, pleasure her with my tongue. She kisses my neck and immediately I am wet for her. Then she walks away and I never see her again.

I am with my lover in a bar and I start flirting with a man across the room – he wants me, and my lover knows he wants

Mark D'Arbanville

me, and I know it too. I move over to the man and he starts talking to me, he buys me a drink, his hand touches the bare skin of my forearm, he whispers something in my ear, his mouth is close to my neck. I start to kiss him and touch him, he is hard already, and I look over his shoulder and watch my lover's face as I stroke him. The three of us leave the bar together. I want him to watch. I want my lover to watch me possessed and pinned by another man.

My lover is with his girlfriend, they are dancing hip to hip and I arrive unannounced. I watch her grind her sex into him, a long slow dance. I can see his erection through his jeans. He knows I am there and our eyes meet across the room and then I start dancing with his friend. I don't even know him but my hips move against him. I see my lover watching me, he is so hot with jealousy and passion and I am on fire for him. We know we have to meet, we have to, we will have to be discreet but . . .

I am a thousand parts, and I am all of them. I drift, I love, I am who I am at any moment, because that is me, and that is how I want to be . . .

I throw the letter on the bed. I can't believe I wrote that. Is this how I want to be? Did I want to be some witch who hurt people and played with their lives and their emotions? I am disgusted with the woman who wrote the letter.

I am also wet.

– I would never do those things.

– No, you wouldn't.

– Then why did you show me this?

– It's the wave inside that's crashing against your sandbags. I may be wrong but I always thought it must be hard work building that dam.

The letter was my secret world, even now. Instead of memories I had dreams, dirty and tender, in my mind I was an actress of a thousand roles. I thought that this was because I had no memories of my own. Now it seems it has always been this way.

– Do you think I would have pursued you like I did, would have waited as long as I did, if it wasn't for letters like this? It's like a secret code, Anna. You sent it to me so many times, in emails and text messages and the things you said. You said you wanted to be normal and conventional but you let me know a hundred different ways that you weren't. It was like a beacon, flashing in the night. Whenever I think I've lost you, you give me a fix again, and I know you're still there, bobbing on the sea, alone in the dark.

– It's just some stupid scribbling.

– I think this letter is why we were together, Anna. We both have secret gardens. Neither of us quite fits in out there, in the world. But maybe I'm wrong.

– I'm happy now. I want to go home to Paul.

He shrugs his shoulders.

I go to the bathroom. I lock the door and slide down the wall onto the cold tile floor.

Who am I really?

Am I the wave or the sandbags that keep it from washing over my life?

Mark D'Arbanville

Fifty-nine

We drive back to London in the gathering of the evening, to my other life. To a life that was mine, yet wasn't mine at all.

I saw what that other Anna might have seen in Mark; he opens car doors, he isn't afraid to touch, or to smile, and sometimes when he looks at me it is as if he can see something in me that I cannot see. It scares me and I want to run away from him. And it fascinates me and makes me want to stay forever.

I have with me the blood-flecked script that Sally rescued from the wreck of the car. I start to read it. I am enthralled by the story, by the beauty of the language he uses and how he captures a character in just a few lines of action or dialogue. He can evoke emotion in a way that sometimes leaves me choked. There is nothing arthouse in what he does; it is raw and candid and passionate and real.

– This is beautiful, Mark. Wonderful. I love the woman in this, she is so . . . you.

I stare at him.

He reaches into the console and finds the letter he showed me in the cottage. He throws it on top of the script. I take another look: *I am a princess . . .*

– I love that woman in the letter. But she comes and she goes. Some days she's there, some days she's not. Fuck knows what I'm going to do about it.

As he put it so earthily: fuck knows what I'm going to do about it either.

Mark D'Arbanville

Sixty

Unravelling, falling apart.

Mark drops me off at Earls Court station and finds me a cab. I kiss him on the cheek, get in the back and ride home to Chelsea, numb and exhausted.

I turn and watch him through the back window, his body heavy with strain and his face drawn and pale and angry and tired. It seems to me I have taken his life and turned it upside down. I didn't know what good things I had brought him, I only knew that once he had had a wife and family and then I changed everything.

I want to sleep forever.

Sixty-one

I take out the diary, hidden in a bottom drawer of my dresser, another secret. I have not opened it since I first found it. I flick through it, my hands shaking. There are more pages glued together at the back. I carefully cut through the outside of the pages and lift them open. The ink is not as faded as it is on the other pages, and written in an adult hand, not the childish scrawl of the rest of the diary.

Dear Guardian Angel,

I said I wouldn't write anymore . . . but that was six years ago now and I found you again. I need to write down how I feel. I don't understand it, all I know is that something happened to me ages ago but I can't work out if it was real or a dream. I mean, I always make up such stories. Or so Dad says.

It is strange that I don't know why I don't like older men touching me. I flinch if someone gets too close to me but perhaps

Mark D'Arbanville

that is just me. Sometimes deep down I question this. Perhaps
something did happen to me. Perhaps I don't make up stories.
  Why would Dad say that I do?

That night I toss and turn. I wake at three in the morning
with my head at the foot of the bed, the bedclothes on the
floor, even the undersheet. I am still awake at dawn light, as
the first traffic starts to hum again on Fulham Road.

I have showered but I can still smell Mark on me. Just my
imagination or is it my guilt? Last night I cheated on Paul;
tonight I will cheat on Mark.

– Hey, Anna.

My eyes blink open. I must have fallen asleep.

– Paul. You're early.

I feel jumpy, distracted. Hard to focus.

He sits on the edge of the bed. He looks so boyishly happy
to see me.

– I wanted to get back as soon as I could. How have you
been? Have you been okay?

His concern for me breaks my heart. He has been worry-
ing about me and I have been cheating on him. I am a bitch.
I hate myself.

Whoever I am.

– I'm fine, sweetheart.

– How was your trip?

I can see in his eyes that he knows. But he won't say. He
will never come right out and ask.

– I remembered something, I say, to distract him, something Mark tells me I do very well.

– I remembered . . . there was a beach house. I remembered a restaurant called Il Cuomo. Did we go there together?

He blinks away a tear. I have done something right. I have made at least one man happy! He sweeps me up in his arms.

– Oh honey, he whispers. You are coming back! You are coming back to me!

For a moment I feel safe. Mark and the letter and the thousand other women are put to the side.

For the moment.

Mark D'Arbanville

Sixty-two

David is home for the holidays. Mark picks him up at the station. They stop off at the supermarket for groceries and David stays in the car. When Mark gets back, his impatient son has locked the car and gone looking for him and locked them both out. The keys are where Mark left them, in the ignition.

– For fuck's sake, what did you do that for? Mark says. David discovers one of the back doors is unlocked, and climbs in.

– See, you didn't have to throw a spastic, he says.

They sit in blistering silence until they are almost home.

– For God's sake, what's wrong?

– It's you, David says. Why do you have to be so angry all the time?

– I wasn't angry. I was frustrated.

– You didn't have to go off like that.

– I didn't go off.

– You could have just said, for fuck's sake. But then you made it personal.

– Because I asked you why you did that?

– I can't do this anymore, David says, and gets out just as they reach the house. He stamps off down the street. Mark parks the car in the garage and goes inside the house to cool down. This is unbelievable. How did we get here?

Well, he's not going to get an olive branch from me this fucking time. I am absolutely right here, no question. There is no way on this earth I am going to say sorry to him this time.

The house is piled with boxes. Mark is packing up the house, moving to a smaller place nearer Manchester. He finds a box full of old photographs and cards. One of them is for David, sent just after his mother's funeral, and it's from friends of Mark's and Susan's. At least he thought they were friends of his.

Dear David,

Just a note to say thinking of you. If we could change the way life turned out for you, we would. You are loved by everyone who loved your mum, and that was many, many people. I hope you can find at least a little bit of strength in that.

Your dad loves you too, he just can't find his own way at the moment, and that makes us all mad at him . . .

He screws up the card and throws it with some force into the litter bin. The condescension is the worst thing. Leave your wife and everyone thinks there's something wrong with

Mark D'Arbanville

you. *Can't find his own way.* What they mean is*: won't live the way we do.* What pricks. It doesn't matter if you're fucking happy or miserable; all that matters is that you conform.

Underneath the card is a hand-scrawled note from David: *Mum don't leave me. Give me a chance to say goodbye. You don't need to do this. What am I going to do without you?*

Oh, for Christ's sake. He just wants to pack up the fucking house and go.

He hears the back door slam. David appears at the study door and stands there. He is looking for the way out, same as Mark.

– David, I'm sorry. I'm sorry I yelled at you.

– It's okay, he says, and shrugs it off.

– No, I mean it, and from nowhere and for no particular reason Mark starts the abseil down, first off his pedestal, and then his high horse. It's a long way down.

– I'm sorry for all the times I yelled at you. Whether it was right or wrong, if I scared you or made you feel bad, then I'm sorry, I really am.

They stare at each other across the yawning chasm of their separate grief.

– You were the bomb as a dad.

– Does that mean I was good or I was terrible?

– You were the best.

Mark is flattered by this summation of his performance. Because he never felt that capable. There is an embarrassed silence.

– I'll bring the bags in out of the car, David says.

– No, wait, Mark tells him.

They look at each other.

– We did have some big fights, didn't we, the last couple of years? David says.

– Yeah. We did.

– You used to get so mad at me.

– I think I was pretty unhappy the last few years. I didn't know just how much. But I didn't have to take it out on you.

Mum don't leave me. Give me a chance to say goodbye. You don't need to do this. What am I going to do without you?

– What's up, Dad? You all right?

– I'm sorry about what happened. It shouldn't have gone down that way. I mean, the separation . . . I screwed it up, everything.

– It wasn't your fault, he says, and then, incredibly: I know you were unhappy. You can't blame yourself.

Mark cannot believe his ears. For over a year David has blamed no one but his father, and he was inclined to agree. This is his absolution. David has forgiven, something Mark never expected him to do.

– You having a hard time? David asks.

Mark shrugs. He wouldn't know where to start.

– You know, it would be all right. If this is about her. I don't mind anymore. If she makes you happy, go for it. I'm cool with all that now.

– Thanks, David. That is a very generous thing to say. But we won't be getting together, I don't think.

– Why aren't you with her?

– I don't know how to begin to explain it all to you.

David thinks about this.

Mark D'Arbanville

– Are you sorry then? That you left Mum?

I shake my head.

– No, David. I don't think you should stay with someone just because they love you. It has to be more than that. There has to be a spark. Whatever spark we had, it had gone.

There is a long silence while they both try and think of something to say. Instead, David does an extraordinary thing. He steps into the room and hugs his father. Not for long and not very close, but for David it is a bold move. He mumbles something about loving him, or Mark thinks that's what he says, and then he is gone from the room.

Mark sits at his desk staring at snow falling listless from a grey sky.

His son is not only back for the holidays. He is back from despair. For today, at least. And if they can do it today, then maybe they can do it another time one other day, and maybe someday soon.

Sixty-three

Sunday lunch. Apparently a tradition where I come from. Paul and I arrive promptly at twelve thirty. There is the smell of a roast from the kitchen. Cathy and her husband Ian are already there. There are smiles and kisses.

Dear Guardian Angel. What the fuck is wrong with this picture? Is this all a sham?

My father, Anna's father, gives me a bear hug. I freeze on the inside. *Dear Guardian Angel. Who is this man?*

– Where's Mum?

– Oh, you know your mother, flapping around somewhere. I never know what she's doing.

I find her in the kitchen, pulling a sizzling pan of roasted potatoes and pumpkin out of the oven. She has a big smile for us. She seems like a wonderfully warm-hearted woman. A bit traditional, perhaps. And the only one who seems to do any real work around the house.

The whole afternoon she never seems to have a moment to

herself. She is always busy putting things in and out of the oven, fetching drinks, making sure everyone is happy. *Making sure everyone else is happy.*

And he just sits there.

Such a needy man. While we eat Mum's roast, the conversation has to revolve around him, his blood pressure, his pigeons, his ranting about politics and the state of the world as he sees it.

– Your mother's no bloody help, he says. She spends all our money on dresses.

I wait for her to say something but she doesn't.

– Is that a new shirt you're wearing? I say. He seems to me to be always immaculately turned out. I have seen my mum in the same dress three times in a row when I was in the hospital.

– Oh don't start, Anna. You haven't forgotten how to be a pain in the arse, have you?

He gets up suddenly and leaves the table, slamming the door on his way out. Just one comment and he is off the edge.

– Don't mind your father, darling, Mum says to me, he has a migraine.

It seems to me my father's life is a constant migraine. And everyone has to have a migraine with him.

It is late in the afternoon, Mum is in the kitchen doing the washing up, Cathy helping her. Paul is watching football on the television with Ian. I finally have a moment alone outside in the garden with this man they call my father.

He is fiddling with the lawnmower. He looks up surprised as I walk into the shed. He seems awkward that I have cornered him, as if he knows what is coming. Since I woke up

I have quickly bonded with my mum; but he and I, we are like strangers.

– Good to see you looking so well, he says. You had us all worried there.

– Dad . . .

And I hesitate, don't know quite how to say this to him.

– Had to go back to the doctor's last week. He's worried about my blood pressure. Says I have to take it easy.

– What was it like, when we were kids?

– Cholesterol's a bit high. Told your mother not to cook with butter all the time but she doesn't listen.

– What was it like when we were growing up?

He stares at me, he hasn't been listening. The question irks him. He has that look on his face: crazy Anna and her daft questions.

– How do you mean? You've heard all the stories a hundred times since you woke up.

It's true. The family lore has been repeated to me over and over as they tried to prise some hidden memory from me.

– Did we have any problems, you know, as a family?

His face is suddenly flushed.

– Of course we didn't. Well, nothing we couldn't handle. Your mother's sister was always flashing all her money around making your mother feel less than, but we were very happy in our way.

– What was I like, as a kid?

A moment's hesitation.

– Your mother's shown you all the photo albums.

– I want to hear it from you.

Mark D'Arbanville

He thinks about this.

— Well, if you really want to know, you were a bit of a rat-bag, always off somewhere in your own head and you would make up the most crazy stories. And you were always flaunting yourself around . . .

Flaunting myself around. What does he mean by that?

— You'd tell these bloody stupid stories. Going around scaring everyone . . .

— Did you ever hit me?

Silence. Then:

— You just got what every little girl gets who is being naughty, that's all. I wasn't having a brat in the house and you were going to end up in trouble if you weren't disciplined now and then. Your sister seemed to fall in line but you were different. Always had an answer for everything! Maybe I gave you a bit of a guiding hand now and then, suppose you might call it. Never did you any harm.

And then, perhaps, he sees my expression and he starts to get angry.

— To be honest, Anna, we were worried for a long time you had something wrong with you! I mean, there was a time you'd come home from school every day and lock yourself in your room and never say anything to anyone. Even your mother started to think you were sick. You'd run away to the side of the house when you didn't get your way, stay there all day with your dolls, God knows what you were doing.

— What do you mean, something wrong with me?

— I don't know. We thought you might be . . .

— You mean mental problems?

– Perhaps.

– And when did you stop thinking that?

A long and aching silence.

Suddenly I am there at the side of the house again, the sun has started to slip down the sky and shadows reach out for me from the wooden fence. It will get cold soon, and I hate the cold.

I have arranged my dolls in a semicircle around me, they are all smiling happily, my perfect little children, perfect, they never get into trouble, not like me. I don't understand why I make up the things I do, I don't understand why I walk in my sleep, why these bad people visit me in my dreams, I don't know what I have done to be punished like this.

I am scared that I am going to die but I will not worry about that now, I will keep this worry until I am old, like eighteen, then I can worry about that. I won't die now. Or will I? The girl down the road died, she died in the park, I don't understand why.

I talk too much, Dad says, I have a smart mouth and I always think I am right. I don't mean to, I must learn to be quiet but it is really hard if I see or hear something that I think is wrong, I have to say something. If I keep doing this nobody will like me.

You need to just say what people want to hear.

I mean, I wrote the story for my English teacher just like she said, even though that wasn't what I really wanted but they thought I did so I fooled them, and I guess I can do that if it makes my life easier, if it makes Mum happy.

I can just say yes to everyone and nod just like my perfect dolls then everyone will be happy with me and if I have other thoughts I can come here and talk to my dolls or write about them, but best to keep those thoughts inside, then I will hurt nobody and I will

Mark D'Arbanville

have friends and people will like me. It would be awful if no one liked me.

I can hear Dad screaming. I put my hands over my ears but his voice seems to cut through anything. I try and stuff bits of grass in my ears so I don't have to listen. Mum is crying, I try and think of something funny to say so she will brighten up but I don't much feel like it today.

But I have to, I have to for Mum. I can make up a story and make her forget about everything and then we will all be okay.

– Anna.

– She is there. My mum is right there, next to me.

– Anna, are you all right?

– Off with the bloody fairies again, Dad says.

I realise with a start I have drifted, just like Mum does. I am there in Dad's shed, and he is staring at me like I am mad, and Mum is standing there in the doorway, smiling like always.

– Anna, I made a cup of tea.

– Lives in a world of her own, Dad says.

– She's still getting better, Mum says.

– Always been the same, he says and goes out.

I stare at my father. I hate him. I feel crazy, alone and frightened. A grown woman now and I want to hide round the corner of the house, with my dolls, with my perfect world, and never let him hurt me again.

Sixty-four

Her plaque is under a chestnut tree in the memorial park. Her memory is proscribed by less than forty years of life, and below her name and the dates there is a small engraving of an elephant. She loved elephants.

Mark sits cross-legged and listens to the wind in the leaves above his head. He wants to talk to her but nothing will come. There is no healing because he is still bleeding, haemorrhaging fucking everywhere.

When a man leaves his wife, you can't ever trust him again. Isn't that what they say? Cheat once and he'll cheat again. Abandon once and he'll abandon again. That's what any woman thinks. You're damned if you do and damned if you don't. Only it wasn't like that.

– I wasn't like that, he says aloud.

But what is the point of trying to explain? No one wants to listen. They have you pegged for this or for that, everyone thinks they know how it is without asking.

Mark D'Arbanville

– Susan, he says aloud.

Why is it so hard to talk to a woman I was married to for fifteen years?

Like most people he had never been able to get out of relationships because he never really knew why he had gotten into them in the first place. Do you marry so you will never have to be alone, so you'll be safe? Insurance against being lonely?

– Sue, oh Suzie. Thank you for my son, for believing in me when no one else did, for all that laughter and love when I was simpler and so different to the man I was later to become. I owed you, I owed you a lot. I suppose by your lights, I let you down.

I thought I loved you.

Or maybe love is what we do when we are crazy. That is the beauty of it. If love is what you do when it makes sense, the chances are it's just rational and not really love.

So do you love someone only if they will love you back? A sense of self preservation tells us to love only when it is safe to do so; when that love can return us the things we want.

He had loved Susan that way; he had always held back a little, had been cool and rational about it, calculating sometimes, in control all the time. He had loved her but not in the way of losing himself in it. Which was what she wanted from him, and what she deserved.

What is there to say to her now?

This is impossible. He gets up and starts to walk back to his car.

Anna.

Just an affair, people will say. It's easy to be in love when it's exciting and new and dangerous.

– Yeah? Well, you fucking try it, he says to the wind. You see how exciting it is, all the goodbyes, the jealousy when she goes back to her husband's bed, every day never knowing if you're going to see her again, the endless recriminations that go hand in hand with the triangulation of love.

Please God, help me stop loving her. I don't want to love her any more! I don't want to feel this way. I want to let her go. She just feels guilty over me, that's all, and that's why I don't want to love her any more. Guilt isn't love and that wasn't what brought us together in the beginning or kept us together through so much heartache.

So much guilt. Guilt most of all for her infidelity. But what is it to be faithful? Is fidelity lack of opportunity, lack of desire? Is fidelity another duty to fulfil? Or do you rather stay faithful to a man, or to a woman, because your passions are served right where you are, because they are enough on their own?

Because you are in love?

But now he wondered if he ever really knew what love was. So how would he know?

Mark D'Arbanville

Sixty-five

Sally is downstairs in the car. She calls up on her mobile to tell me she is waiting. I am so excited. We are going out for dinner. I feel like I have just been let out of school.

– Are you sure you don't want me to pick you up? Paul asks.

– I'll be fine, I'll get a taxi home, don't worry.

– Anna, don't drink too much, you know that –

– I know, I know, alcohol is the enemy. I promise I won't have too many, okay? We'll alternate drinks with water. I just want to dance. I've remembered how much I loved to dance!

I run out of the door into the crisp chill of the evening. I am free. I am going to go out and have fun and not worry about Paul or Mark or babies or even who I am. I can just be me.

When we get to the restaurant I order champagne.

– Anna . . .

– I know. Paul doesn't like me drinking. But won't it be

better if I start drinking now and then by the time I get home I'll be sober?

Sally shrugs her shoulders and laughs.

The waiter brings the champagne. He pours the Veuve into two crystal flutes and leaves the bottle in the ice bucket.

– Sally, there's something I have to ask you, something I have to know.

– Shoot.

– Were there any other affairs, I mean, beside Mark?

– Anna, you tell me everything, and there's been nothing like Mark. There probably never will be again, nothing will rock you like that. It just seemed impossible to stop. You could easily have walked away from each other countless times. But you couldn't. You were so drawn to each other.

I feel a load lift off my shoulders. Every man I met, I wondered if I had slept with them. I wanted to know I wasn't a slut, that Mark was special.

– Did I talk to you much about it? About me and Paul and about Mark?

– You used to say that Paul worked for you in the beginning because he was so remote and it was a challenge to make him love you. And he liked to be looked after and you said you liked doing that. It was all about him – if he was happy then so were you.

– Was I happy?

– If you were happy, there wouldn't have been Mark.

– What did I tell you about him?

Sally smiles.

– I remember the week you met him. You said he came

into your life like a hurricane. You thought because he had a wife it wouldn't lead to anything more. Even though I think a part of you really wanted it to. It sounded to me like Mark was happy to play the role of the lover, at first. But then he tore up the script. I remember you said to me, how could you trust his love for you if he left his wife?

— It's true, isn't it? How could he trust me either?

Sally doesn't answer.

— Isn't that the way it goes? I would be knocked off that pedestal, he would see me as I am, and how long would the spark last then? He'd get bored with me. All men do.

Am I trying to convince Sally or myself? I'm right, of course, seen it so many times. But what if I'm not? What if this really was something rare, like Sally said?

— You lived on adrenalin before the accident.

— There you are then. I was just in love with the drama.

I wish Sally would say something.

— But why Mark? I ask her.

— You said you loved him because he could somehow release a part of you that you kept hidden away, a place you only went to in your writing and in your dreams. You said you hated him for the same reason, because he wanted you to bring those dreams into the real world. You said it was too risky, that it could destroy you.

— It's like, if we are finally together then it makes all his pain and suffering justified. He's so sure I hold the key for him, but how can I trust that? Especially now. I feel suffocated and out of control and I hate this, I feel as though I am trapped in a corner.

I drain my glass and pour another. We drink two bottles of champagne between us and afterwards, instead of going home, we go to a nightclub in Soho.

And damn him. He is there.

Mark D'Arbanville

Sixty-six

His hand is holding hers, and he leans over the table to kiss her. I feel like I am going to be sick. He did not mention her to me at the cottage when he was telling me how much I fucked up his life and how special we were together.

I feel weak. A part of me is saying: *well, this is good, he is happy, I have Paul, and everything is going to be all right. We can all go back to our other lives and everything will be fine.*

Another part of me wants to cut off his balls.

– Anna, what's the matter, did you see a ghost?

– Mark is over there. He has a woman with him.

– Oh my God. Of all the nightclubs, in all the world, he has to pick this one!

It's a line from *Casablanca*. Sally is trying to make me laugh. It doesn't work.

– Have you seen him since he stormed off in his car?

– No, I lied. I hate lying to Sally but I can't cope with my infidelity being aired again. I don't feel so guilty if it is just my secret.

I wonder why I feel better if no one else knows. Is it about what I do or about what my friends and family think of me?

We order vodkas, and I drain my glass. There is a weight in my chest. I want to throw up my dinner. How can I be jealous when I don't remember anything about him, about us, when I have a husband at home that I love?

He still hasn't seen me. They are drinking red wine. I hate red wine. She is laughing too loud at his jokes, flicking her long dark hair over her shoulder. I can't do that anymore. It is too short now.

– I'm going to the bathroom, I tell Sally.

I don't need to. I just can't sit there and watch them.

I stand in front of the wall mirror in the washroom, staring at this crazy woman, her mascara streaked down her face. Insanely jealous of a man she said she didn't love.

And suddenly she is there right next to me. Mark's new girlfriend. Checking her make-up and smiling at me in the mirror.

– I love your top.

I can't fucking believe this.

– Thanks.

– Having a good night?

– I guess.

I feel like an idiot. I can't even string a sentence together.

– Are you here with a friend? I ask her.

– I met this gorgeous man when I was in Spain, she says, applying her lip gloss. Fucked him once and thought that would be it. Couldn't stop thinking about him when I got back. He is just the most amazing man I ever met. And a complete sex god.

Mark D'Arbanville

She is drunk. Why else would she be rambling like this to a complete stranger?

I feel sick. I rush into one of the cubicles and bring up my dinner. Jealousy is ripping me apart. It doesn't make any sense. I don't want him, I want Paul.

Don't I?

Last week he made love to me and tonight he is with that bitch out there. He has known her for five minutes. Perhaps he made love to her that morning before he picked me up. If he is so fucking happy why does he want to see me again?

When I come out of the cubicle she is gone. I rinse my mouth out in the sink. I rejoin Sally at the bar. Miss Hair Flicker is sitting on his lap, practically screwing him right there on the banquette.

– Sally, let's go.

Sally already has her bag over her shoulder.

– Do you want to go home?

– No, I just want to dance. Somewhere Mark is not going to show up with Julia Roberts.

As we rush out into the night, I glance back over my shoulder. He still hasn't seen me. His hands are all over her, on her hip, on her thigh. He brushes a wisp of hair from her cheek, gentle and loving as he used to do to me.

As he used to do to me.

Now how do I know that? How do I remember that? Why am I jealous of a stranger I do not even know unless deep down I do remember something of us? I feel another boiling rush of jealousy in my veins. I want to go over and say, I hope you'll be very happy together, the two of you. Strange how in all his moralising at the cottage he had forgotten to mention Miss Open Legs.

Sally sees me hesitate, must divine what I am thinking, and drags me out of the door and into the cold night air.

We go to a club in Chelsea and I drink way too much and dance way too long. I forget about him and I forget about her. I almost forget about him and I almost forget about her. I nearly pass out in the taxi going home. When I get through the door I rip off my clothes and jump on top of Paul, who is asleep in our bed.

I tug hard on his soft penis and put my tongue in his mouth and on his penis until he is hard, then I put him inside me and I want to come, I want it to be great and passionate, sweat and come everywhere, but it's not because I am too drunk to feel anything. Then I am crying and he is holding me in his arms, saying what's the matter, baby, and then I roll him on top of me again and I want him to fuck me and I want him to be Mark. I fall asleep – I don't know if it is before or after we finish.

To his credit, he does not seem to mind. When I wake up, my mouth gummy and dry and my head hammering with pain, he is asleep under my arm.

My baby. I love him. But just not quite the way I want to.

Mark D'Arbanville

Sixty-seven

A text: *Desperate to see you. I love you.*

I want to throw the phone at the wall.

I text back: *Will you bring your girlfriend with you?*

God, was he always such a good liar? How many women did he have affairs with over the years? Was I just another notch on that long thick bedpost?

Ten minutes pass between beeps.

We need to talk.

I don't answer. God, but I want him to text me again. Please text me again.

Half an hour later: *I need to explain please let me explain.*

We arrange to meet at a café in Fulham Palace Road. I am seething with anger. My jealousy has overtaken me. This is insane. I have a husband I love very much, Mark can sleep with whoever he wants, I should be really happy for him. What is this madness? What is happening to me?

We could be friends. And I could be friends with her, too.

Mark walks in through the door. And it is like a bolt of electricity passes between the two of us. Neither of us speaks. He sits down in the chair opposite and we stare at each other for an eternity. Finally:

– Anna, is this about Maddy?

I hate him. I hate him to my bones. I feel cold, impenetrable. Where is all my resolve to be happy for him, to be friends with his new girlfriend?

– Are you jealous, finally?

– I am not jealous. I hate jealousy. You know that.

– So you keep telling me. But now perhaps you know how I feel.

I want to throw my coffee at him.

– You kept telling me to move on with my life. You kept pushing me away. You kept telling me to find someone who could give you one hundred per cent. You told me you would never ever leave Paul. It was all bullshit, wasn't it? It's so convenient you don't remember any of that now. You are so full of crap, Anna!

I run outside. He follows me. We are getting good at making scenes in the street.

He grabs me and spins me around.

– You seemed pretty happy with how things turned out last night! I say. Why didn't you tell me about her before we went to the cottage?

I am screaming at him. I try to scratch his face and he grabs my arms and holds them tight.

– I love you, I love you but you wanted to stay with Paul. That's what you said you fucking wanted! I'm just trying to get over you. She's great but she isn't you. At least she doesn't torture me night after night by telling me how wonderful I am and then fucking someone else. I hate it, and I hate you for loving me so much you can be fucking jealous and still tell me to love someone else!

He is panting. His eyes are crazy. What am I doing?

I watch myself like I am floating above us, looking at us down there in the wet London street. Now I know he doesn't love her like he loves me, I feel myself detach.

– She loves you, Mark. She thinks you're amazing. You should go to her. Forget about me.

Mark grabs me and pushes me against the wall. I am scared now. Paul would never do this to me. But then I never want to fuck Paul the way I want to fuck Mark.

– It's okay when you're in control, when you're the one with two lovers. But when you have to imagine me in bed with someone else, it's different. Now you know what it was like for me, knowing you were sleeping with Paul every night.

He presses hard against me and kisses me. I kiss him back hungrily, my face wet with tears. The electricity between us is unbearable. I hold his face so hard I want to eat him, squeeze him, kill him. He devours my body through my clothes. We are so wrong for each other and yet why does it feel so right?

Sixty-eight

Mark tosses in his bed, kicks off the sweat-damp sheets. His eyes are gritty. Too tired to get up, unable to lie still. He looks at the luminous dial on his watch. Three seventeen.

Her and Paul. In Paris.

Sex had never been that good for them before, she said. Once a month if she was lucky. Afterwards it seemed they got back on track. Paul should at least have sent him a thank you card and a bottle of twelve year old whisky.

Had she shown him how to use his tongue, where to lay his fingers more gently? Did she use her mouth and hands on him as with him? Was there strip poker, melted chocolate, whispered fantasies, all the delirious and dirty games they had invented together? Did she look deep into his eyes when he came, Mark wondered, as she did with me?

Did they talk for hours afterwards, as she had once done with him? Did she find with Paul the same abandonment and freedom? Did she write, create, lose herself?

Here is the geography of jealousy. He hated himself for it. But he was human, he was just a man, and this had torn out his soul. He didn't want to own her. But Paul had been with her for twelve years and when Mark had met her she was in pieces.

If he hadn't fallen in love with her, against the plan, it wouldn't have mattered. She could have got control of the marriage again, they would have had a nice time, and everything would have been perfect for a few more years.

Right from the first, from the very first, he had said to her: all Paul ever has to do is stick around, refuse to leave, and you will lose the will for change, for really fundamental change. He will wear you down.

What business was it of his? He should have walked away then. He had said to her: *I don't want to be the one who makes him realise what a fool he has been.*

But she can't remember that now. She could barely remember it before.

Who was she really? Did he fall in love with a woman who was just bored and looking for an affair, or a woman looking to profoundly change her life?

What should it matter to me?

Sixty-nine

Another Sunday lunch at my parents' house.

Paul is away on work. My mother is inside washing the dishes and Ian is helping her. Cathy and I are talking in the back garden, a grim grey winter afternoon, the drone of a 747 overhead. I can see my father through the French windows, sitting on the lounge, watching television with his bottle of beer.

Since reading the diaries, I have had a bad feeling whenever I am around him.

– I saw Mark last week.

There is a long silence.

– Did you hear me?

– I heard you. I just hoped I heard you wrong.

– I hoped you might . . . understand.

– Do you really want to go through all of that again? He's no good for you. You're a married woman, for God's sake.

– He loves me.

– Sure, they all love you, until the next one comes along. He cheated on his wife, he can cheat on you!

– Keep your voice down!

She takes a breath and then hisses at me:

– Are you out of your mind? which I think is a pretty insensitive thing to say. I can see by the look on her face that she immediately regrets it.

– I just need some time to sort things out in my head.

– That is what you always say. What you always said! You never got sorted! Not ever! You are so fucking selfish, Anna. You always were. Something else you've conveniently forgotten about.

– What do you mean?

– Paul is wonderful. He loves you and he gives you everything you want! But you want the best of both worlds, don't you?

I cannot believe the look of disgust on her face. She is my sister. Isn't she supposed to love me, isn't she supposed to understand?

– If you just wanted to fuck someone . . . Why does it have to be an affair? You don't remember this now, but you would be at my house in tears every time you saw him, every time you broke up. I don't remember how many times I sat up with you at night listening to you pour your heart out! Every time you said you were going to end it!

She is shouting again. I steal a guilty glance back at the house. Oh, fuck. Dad is standing there, staring at us, and there is this look on his face, and it scares me. I put my hand on Cathy's arm to warn her.

I wonder how much he has heard.

– Cathy, can you leave us on our own for a minute, please, he says.

Cathy looks scared. I don't want her to go. I wonder if I am about to see the father I read about in my ballerina diary. She jumps to her feet and rushes inside the house.

– What's this about?

– Nothing. It's girl talk.

– It sounded to me like you were being a little slut again.

I cannot believe the name he has just called me. Mark said I'd told him I had had just three men in my whole life. Three men. Does that make me a slut? I don't think so.

– Are you having an affair?

– This is none of your business.

– Well I'm making it my business. Who is this man? Is this someone you met since you got out of hospital?

I get to my feet.

– I'm not discussing it with you.

– You always were the flirty type. Always wanted to be the centre of attention. I told your mother you'd end up in trouble one day.

He takes a step closer and I can smell the beer on his breath.

– What is wrong with you? Can't you keep your legs closed?

I feel my skin crawl. I feel suddenly paralysed. I am a grown woman, I am taller than he is now, but suddenly I feel as if I am five years old. I want to run inside the house away from this appalling man but my legs won't move.

– Don't talk to me like that! You don't even know me. You know nothing about me.

Mark D'Arbanville

– I could tell you a thing or two. You are sleeping around, aren't you? I knew this would happen one day.

– I'm not going to let you do this anymore!

I hate him so much I can barely get the words out. My throat closes over. The fear and hate pump through me like poison. I feel small and afraid and alone. And I feel so weak. How has this happened? How has this man made me feel like this with just a look and a few words, when I can't even remember anything, when all I have is a few scribbled lines in an old diary?

– You don't control me! I scream at him, but he does control me, somehow he knows how to make me feel like this.

– Have you been sleeping around?

– My life is my affair.

His face twists into a look of pure disgust.

– You little tramp.

He slaps me hard, once, across the cheek. The blow sends me reeling back. I can't breathe. I feel tears stinging my eyes and the metallic taste of my own blood in my mouth. The whole side of my face is numb.

I run into the house to fetch my bag. I just want to get out of that house, get out and never come back. My mother and Cathy have been watching from the window and they just stare, neither of them knowing what to do. And him, he's followed me inside. I want him to get away from me, he is not going to touch me again, not ever. I see the big knife lying on the draining board on the kitchen sink, the one Mum uses to carve the Sunday roast. I pick it up.

– Don't come near me.

– What do you think you're going to do with that?

– You are never ever going to touch me again.

– Darling. Don't! It's Mum, she is standing right there behind me. She is white and her fists have gone to her mouth.

– I told you this is how she'd turn out, he says to her. Do you know what she's been up to? Do you?

She doesn't answer him.

– Always off in her own little world! She still bloody is! Tramp!

– Leave her be, George.

He takes a step towards me and tries to take the knife away. I take a step back, and slash out at him. He yelps like a beaten dog and grabs at his forearm. Blood oozes through his fingers like little red worms and starts to drip on the ground.

– You cut me, he says. She cut me, he repeats, staring at my mother.

– Don't you ever call me that again. Don't you ever, ever, call me that name again. You are never going to hurt me again!

He is whimpering. She cut me, he keeps saying over and over. And when he looks up I see something in his face that the little girl who wrote the diary would never have seen.

Fear.

I drop the knife on the lino and push past Ian, who is standing there, eyes wide, in the kitchen doorway. I grab my bag and my car keys and run out of the house.

Mark D'Arbanville

Seventy

The room is dark and cold. I creep out of bed and go to the study. Scripts, contracts lie everywhere. All from before the accident. They tell me this is what I did. I wonder if I will work again.

I catch my reflection in the mirror. I stare into my eyes, willing my soul to give me some answers, willing myself to not want to see Mark again.

There is a letter opener on the desk. I start to rub it against my wrist. I hate myself, who I was, who I am. The blade starts to bite in, but it doesn't even hurt. I feel completely disconnected. Blood drips off the end of my fingers onto the desk. I watch fascinated as it drops in red spots onto the page of a script. *Infidelity*. The script Mark said he and I had written together.

When I look back at the mirror Susan is standing there. Her cheeks are hollowed and she is ashen in death.

– You took everything I wanted. How could you do this to me?

– I didn't do anything. It wasn't my fault.

– You destroyed my family. You destroyed my life. I want you dead for what you did. I want you to pay.

I feel the warm flow of blood down my fingers, down my arms, onto the carpet, onto the script, onto the desk. It doesn't hurt at all. No pain, just guilt pouring out of me. I should hurt. I deserve to hurt.

– I didn't know, I didn't ask him to love me.

– You planned this from the very start. You're a slut. You don't even love him, you're already married. Isn't one man enough for you? Everything comes so easy to you, doesn't it, now you have my husband and I fucking want him back.

– What do you want me to do?

– I want you to tell him you don't love him, that it was just sex, you didn't ever love him, tell him he means nothing to you. Tell him!

– But you're gone now. How can you get him back?

– It's the only way you can make amends. The only way he can make amends. Do you understand?

She takes off her wedding ring and hurls it at my face.

– Nobody likes you, you know that, don't you? You have no real friends. What kind of woman would do this to another woman? You have to make this right.

– How?

– You have to suffer, like I did.

There is blood everywhere. How can there be so much? I tear off my t-shirt and wrap it around my wrist so I don't make any more mess. I feel like she is reaching through the mirror to strangle me. There is no air in the room. Everything is spinning . . .

Mark D'Arbanville

I fall against the desk. I see writing in the margins of the script Mark gave me, the one from the car wreck: *The rumours and accusations have started, there's a few people in the industry who know, people avoid my eyes now, people are talking about it, making up stories, no one knows the whole truth. I have no one to talk to about this. I don't expect anyone to really understand. His friends all blame me* . . . I look back in the mirror. She is still there.

– You're going to pay for this, she says.

She is right. I have to pay. It is the only way I can make up for what I did. I have to pay and make Mark see I never loved him, not ever, and go back to Paul and make a decent life, find my redemption in being a good woman again.

Blood is seeping through the t-shirt and onto the floor and my wrist is hurting now, a deep throbbing ache, and I stumble back to the bedroom. I feel too weak to stand anymore.

– Paul, I murmur. I think I've cut myself, I say, and then everything goes black.

Seventy-one

– **Anna.**

Paul is sitting next to the bed, looking sad and so very tired.

– What happened?

He does not answer and then I remember the letter opener and Susan's face in the mirror, then nothing. God. Now everyone will know, there will be a queue of men in white coats lined up outside the door. How would Mark feel about this?

– You're in hospital, sweetheart. Do you remember now?

– Who knows that I am here?

– Just me sweetheart. No one else.

– I don't want anyone else to know. Please. Don't let anyone else know.

– Okay. It's okay. I won't tell anyone.

– I didn't do this deliberately. I didn't mean to. I want to live. I do. I am so very sorry.

Mark D'Arbanville

There is a flicker of a smile but he does not seem convinced.

– I will do whatever you want, see whoever they want me to see. I just don't want Mum or Dad or anyone else to know, okay, please? I didn't want to die. I absolutely did not, I was just, I don't know what I was doing, and absolutely . . .

– Absolutely?

Absolutely Mark must never know, I think. I look down at my bandaged wrist.

– I want to go home, Paul. Can you take me home?

– I'll talk to the doctors.

He puts his face onto my lap and starts to cry. Once again, I have managed to hurt those who love me in the most despicable way possible. Everything is spiralling out of control.

Seventy-two

I meet him for the last time in Coffee Republic. I am wearing long sleeves that hide the bandage on my wrist.

I am early. He arrives right on time.

He smiles and sits down.

– You look beautiful.

I feel that familiar heat move through me. I don't know how to respond. I do not feel beautiful but Mark has this uncanny ability to make me feel that I am a princess.

– I tried to call you the other night but your phone was off.

– I forgot to charge it.

He knows I am lying but he lets it slide. I am grateful for that.

I tell him I am going away for a while. The clinic is in the mountains near Como. Paul's mother has arranged everything.

I tell him I can have no contact with anyone. He can write letters, but there is no email, no phones. The hospital will update my family of my progress. It sounds like being in prison. Or in a mental home. But I have decided this is my way out of the abyss and the endless cycle of pain. I stare at the table while I tell him the rules.

– This is going to be what I need, I finish, and then start to cry.

I finally look up and I think he might be angry or be crying too, but for once I cannot read his expression.

– Okay.

– That's it. Okay?

– You have said goodbye to me so many times, Anna, one more time just doesn't seem to make that much difference.

He runs a hand across his face.

– I have to remember, I tell him.

– Why?

– I have to find out who I am.

– And you think just remembering things will tell you that?

He looks out of the window at the Austin taxi cabs and the buses moving up and down Gloucester Road.

– How's Maddy?

He looks at me as if I have thrown a glass of cold water over him. A part of me really doesn't want to know. But a part of me does.

– She is fine.

– Won't it be better for you and her if you can sort stuff out without me being around?

– Oh, fuck off.

Wow. He is cold, a million miles away.

– Anna, I have to go. He throws a business card on the table. Here's my address. Write me and I'll write back. Don't forget, he says, and gives a crazy laugh.

He leaves without a hug, without a kiss, a goodbye, anything. I feel stripped of every emotion. I sit there mesmerised for a while and then I walk out. It is a clear cool day and I decide to walk to Hyde Park. But as I cross at the lights I see Mark's car, and he is just sitting there behind the wheel staring straight ahead.

I knock on the driver's side window.

– Mark?

He opens the door and I throw my arms around him.

And then he pushes me away, slams the car into gear and drives off.

Mark D'Arbanville

Seventy-three

He watches her recede in the rear vision mirror.

So she is gone to reclaim her memories. But is that who we are? he wonders. Are we the sum total of our memories? Are we what makes us safe in a life that will end in less than a hundred years? Or are we our passions, and our desires, that last perhaps for as long as our soul moves through this body, through countless bodies, through countless lives?

Is she her husband, her family? Do they define who Anna is?

Are any of us just the sum total of the baggage we collect in our mad rush through our lives?

Or are we all ugly ducklings trying to find which nest we really came from before we were born?

If we forget who we are, can we be recreated from photograph albums and by people telling us what food we liked, what we did, and who we loved? Are we defined by who says they loved us?

How many people had he met in his short life who had yearned to paint, to act, and had never followed that dream because they thought they were too ordinary, too poor, too plain, too . . . scared?

So who is Anna? Is she her city, her job, her family? Is she at the call of those who love and surround her?

This is the testing of every life. And in Anna it has finally reached its apogee.

Mark D'Arbanville

Seventy-four

What I want

To be crazy
To be calm
To be reckless and free and abandoned
To feel safe
A house
To be tender, to touch and kiss and caress as well as drive a man
absolutely crazy with desire, to challenge him physically and
emotionally, this would be the ultimate
A baby very much but perhaps not quite now thank you
A man who loves me in a cerebral but not very physical way, so
that I will always feel in control
A man who feels passionate about life and love and living
A man who will give me a lot of physical and emotional distance
A man with a soul longing and yearning to be matched with
another

A man who does not want to get too close to me
A man who will protect me and keep me safe
A man to nurture, to look after, someone who will rely on me
A romantic, someone I can laugh with, flirt with, and travel with
An intellectual
*Someone passionate, who will make me feel like I am the most
    beautiful woman in the world*
A man who can cry and laugh easily
Someone who is not too emotional
To feel the safety and comfort of what is familiar to me
*To feel like a piece of me fits somehow, somewhere, with somebody
    else and I just know when this does happen – fireworks of
    pain, love, passion will follow and I will know what love and
    living is really about, and I will work out more of me and
    what this woman is.*

Mark D'Arbanville

Seventy-five

Mum is stretched out on the sofa in front of the television, her feet wrapped in her slippers and her glasses crooked on her nose. I do this too. I am often asleep long before the credits roll.

She has come to stay with us for my last night in England before I fly to Como. In the short time I have known her, these few months I have come out of the coma, I have come to admire her so much. The way she lives is so selfless. But it is also clear to me that she has let so much be taken away from her. Everyone else comes first.

Is this another way I am like her? Have I learned too well at my mother's knee?

I have grown fond of her, come to love, a second time. I want her to be happy, and most times I like to think she is happy. She takes pleasure in small things. But sometimes I see this terrible sadness and there is a part of me that wants to take her pain away.

I snuggle onto the lounge and instinctively put my head on her chest. Her arm comes around me and I feel so safe and warm.

She wakes with a start.

– Anna, how long have you been there? What time is it?

– It's midnight.

– I must have dozed off, she says.

And for no reason that I can think of, I start to cry.

– Anna. Sweetheart. What is it?

– I don't want to die, Mum. And I am scared you are going to die as well. What am I going to do if you die?

Where did this come from, this feeling, those words? What am I saying? I feel like I am ten years old again. I have pushed this fear away nearly all my life but it waits there in the darkness in the back of my brain like a mugger.

She holds me in her arms and rocks me. I feel safe here and I fall asleep. But I am not even safe in my dreams for my demons follow me there, through sleep's dark and silent gate.

It's only the secret garden where I'm safe, safe from this fear of dying, of that dark angel called death.

But I know he's out there waiting, for my mum, and for me.

Mark D'Arbanville

Seventy-six

Paul drives me to the airport. I want to tell him how much I love and cherish him but it is all too rushed and tense and the time doesn't seem right.

At the airport he holds on to me so tightly and I respond.

– It is going to be okay, Paul. Whether I find any more of my memories or not, I'll come back better and stronger and ready to move on with our lives, okay?

Why did I say that? If everything is preordained, why am I going to Como and this expensive clinic? If I had already made up my mind, why did I have to go through this endless cycle of pain and turmoil?

– I . . . I love you, Anna. I am a terrible letter writer. But for you I will make the exception, you have always been my exception.

He was squeezing me so hard I thought my spine would break.

– I haven't said this to you since you woke up from the

coma but we didn't have a perfect marriage, Anna, we had many very rough times, a lot of them caused by me . . . I didn't want to love you so damn much. I am selfish, I know it, I locked you out. You were desperate for me and I froze you out. This accident, when I thought you could be gone from my life forever, I kept playing over in my head so many things that have happened, the good, the great and the very bad, and I realised how special you are and how I never want to lose you again. I am not good at talking about how I feel, I hardly know how to say these things, but I am trying to change, if you can give me another chance . . .

I do not know what to say to him. I break away and hurry towards the departure gates.

It is so unlike him to talk this way, he has to be pushed to the limit, while Mark seems to find it so easy to say what is on his mind.

And Mark knows something about my past, something that brings him even closer to me, he knows something he is not telling me. Or even if he does spell it out he knows I will deny it, for I cannot have a man take control over me.

In that way, he feels safe. He knows where my bodies are buried, all of them, past and present, and I know he will never tell anyone. He has this intuitive reading of me which is weirdly reassuring. But on the flip side he is dangerous, passionate and temperamental.

What I treasure more than anything is his friendship. But how do you separate friendship from sexual attraction? Would Mark still be a friend to me if I didn't sleep with him? And if I didn't see him again it would probably be all right – but how

Mark D'Arbanville

would I not want to sleep with him if he walked into the room, if he was sitting next to me right now? Our friendship and our sexuality are both meshed into one and I am desperate to untangle them. The thought of losing him as my confidant is unbearable to me.

But what about Paul? If I choose Mark, what could I say to Paul? I do love Paul, but it is so different. He is the man I had always known I would marry. There was comfort in knowing we would always be together and what the future would be like. He would be a kind husband, I would have a home near family and friends, there would be children and I would have made good, away from the working class roots I had worked so hard to escape. It was the life I had always dreamed of, the life I'd wanted to live.

Mark is dangerous, passionate, a huge risk. I don't like risk. He has had so many women, why would he stop with me? What happens when the muse is replaced, when he finds inspiration and passion with another woman? Wasn't that what happened with his wife? What must it be like to be someone's inspiration and then be replaced, like a Hollywood starlet who is told she is too old and no longer beautiful enough to connect with the audience.

And so the battle goes on between my heart and my head, the risk taker and dreamer in me believing he will love me forever and never leave me no matter what, the more rational part of me colder, harder, reminding me that he is older, wiser, he'll get tired of me soon. I'll fall off my pedestal and then where will I be? I'll irritate him once he's there with me, the intrigue and the mystery will be gone, won't it?

How can he know there will be no other woman for him? Everyone changes. He can't give me for better or worse, richer or poorer, he has already done that and it didn't work. The truth is that nobody would ever be able to give me that anyway. But Paul, well, he and I have survived through everything so far and he is my rock, he is safe and I think perhaps I am enough for him now.

Of course I can't be sure.

Why do my moods change so fast? How could I want to be with both of them? Why can't I make a choice? But what do you do if you just can't, if you search the bottom of your soul, if you beat your hands till they bleed, if you drink three bottles of champagne and the choice is still not clear, what do you do?

What you do is go to what you know, what you have always known.

There is something tucked inside my handbag. Mum gave me a card before I left, and I remember it now and open it. There is a picture of a butterfly on the front of the card. As I open it a letter falls out. I suppose it is from her, but I do not recognise the handwriting. It is faded, and I look at the date at the top; the letter was written thirty-five years ago, *Dearest Amanda*.

Amanda, my mother's name. Fuck. It is not from Mum, it is a letter someone wrote to her. I know, of course, who it must be.

Mark D'Arbanville

Dearest Amanda

I cannot explain how I am feeling tonight, the depth of my loss. Why did this have to happen? Why can't you talk to me anymore? Why can't we be together? I have heard about the pregnancy, I know that wasn't what you expected so soon and you feel you have no choice now. But you still do have a choice! You can still leave, you can make a life with me, we can run away from everyone, everything, I will raise the child as my own. Your baby doesn't have to mean the end to us, it could be the beginning.

Can we meet at the usual place again please, say you will come!

I suppose I know deep in my heart that you won't. If you can't, I will have to leave and go far away. I can't bear to see you and not have you with me. I love you Mandy, I will always love you.

Richard xx

So. We were the reason she stayed! It wasn't about money or security or that she loved Dad more. It was because she was pregnant with Cathy, she was trapped, she didn't have the strength to leave and we were the cause of it. She gave us life, but it took away any choices in hers. She let go of Richard because of us. I guess now I understood why everything was about us kids and what we were doing. We were what she had sacrificed her life for.

I didn't want this, so then what was this strange compulsion in me to imitate her life? She loved my dad, and I know he needed her, but was this why she always looked so sad?

Was this the way it has to be? Is life about sacrifice? Is this what it means to be a mother, to be good?

Over France the plane hits turbulence and bucks through the sky like a runaway horse. I close my eyes and grip the armrests of my seat. Let me die, let me live. Which is it to be?

The turbulence is soon behind us, but I am still holding my breath. The seatbelt sign pings off. In less than an hour we will be landing in Rome. I am afraid of where this journey will lead but part of me also feels a sense of release. Where I am going nobody knows me and nobody wants or needs anything from me. I have no expectations of anyone and no one has any expectations of me.

Mark D'Arbanville

Seventy-seven

— I need a wee, she shouts as she jumps out of bed. She holds her hands behind her as she dashes into the bathroom. Don't look at my bottom, I've got cellulite!

Yellow sun streams through the bedroom window. A better day than he has remembered for a while. Last night as they made love she bit his chest. A different experience to have bruises on the outside of the sternum. She has also bitten the muscle of his shoulder. In the mirror it looks like a smiley face.

Maddy is back in his life. One phone call was all it took.

She tells him her secrets as all women do. You are safe, they tell him. It's why she will leave him in the end. Sometimes she squeezes him too hard, overcome with feelings she cannot contain. She leaves fingernail marks in his butt.

— You are the most amazing man I ever met, she whispers. I am so lucky I ever met you.

And he believes this means more than what it says. As if he didn't learn the first time.

– Thank you, God, she says, grinning as they run along the river in the mornings.

– Thank you, God, she says when he opens the car door for her. Thank you, God, as they lie in bed, sweat cooling on their bodies.

– I've never been good at relationships, she says in the quiet dark. I don't know that anyone has ever loved me. Only my mum. I don't know what it's like.

She tells him no other man has kissed her like this, or touched her as gently. No other man has made her come on her back, she is always on top. No other man has made her come with his tongue over and over. An email one morning in his inbox: *Last night was the most erotic experience of my life.*

Before him, she preferred making love on her own. Her massager was more effective than any man. It is better to go solo. And he recognises this woman, only too well, he knows what he has to do to drive her away, should the need arise. All he has to do is love her and she'll run.

She'll run like fuck.

She is blonde, beautiful. But one night in bed she confesses that one leg is slightly larger than the other. A defect from birth. It is why she only ever wears jeans.

– It doesn't matter, he tells her, and he means this. You are beautiful. No one can notice.

But she doesn't want to be flawed. She has to be untouchable, unhurtable. And he is starting to break down walls.

She wants to know all about Anna, of course.

– You're not over her, are you? she says.

And he says:

– Yes, yes, I am, but it's more hope than reality. He wants to be over her, he doesn't want to love someone who doesn't want him, he doesn't want a woman who wants to throw him out of her life to be the one special woman he has ever loved, he doesn't want that to be the truth.

But it is.

Maddy tells him about a little girl on her first day at school hiding behind a tree when the other children were playing; she had to be coaxed out by a teacher. The girl who was so clingy and needy once has promised herself she will not ever be hurt again. He is in love with another survivor, but survivors know only how to survive. Love means risk and the little girl behind the tree is never going to risk again.

He gets a text message: *I just lubs ya xxx.*

He panics. There is a tenderness for this tough little street fighter that he did not expect. This is meant to be fun, a holding pattern while he sorts his life. But somewhere out there is a woman who loves him and she will not live or die. Her name is Anna and she thinks he is the most special man in the world while she sleeps with someone else. She is the woman who may one day remember she loved him or may never come back to life again.

So he panics and drives her away. He is smarter now, he is not the innocent he once was. He drives her away by telling her he loves her. It scares her to death. He knows from loving Anna that Maddy will run if he tries to get too close, and because he is duplicitous he will now let her hurt him before he hurts her.

Seventy-eight

The clinic looks like a day spa for the rich and famous. I sit on my bed and stare through the windows at the mountains.

I write a letter to Paul, quickly followed by another to Mark. They are both such different letters. I stare at one, then the other. I can hardly believe they are written by the same woman. I wonder if this is how I was, both these men bring out such different things in me.

Dear Paul,

I have arrived safely. Your mother was right. The clinic is more like a five star hotel.

I am really sorry, Paul, for everything that I have put you through. I know the last few months have been terrible and that my moods have been all over the place but it is just so hard trying to remember how I felt or what I did, and what I liked,

Mark D'Arbanville

what I didn't like. I have keenly felt the burden of everyone's expectations.

I loved Paris, I really did, you even let me drink champagne and you didn't say anything. I wanted to tell you that you were wonderful.

I do miss you, Paul, I really do, something inside of me reminds me that I loved you very much.

I suppose Cathy has told you what happened with my dad. It wasn't an accident. I have this intense hatred inside me, I want to let go of it, but it is hard, I am so full of anger sometimes and I don't know why. That cut I have on my lip, I didn't fall like I told you, he hit me – he hit me hard across the face – and it wasn't the first time but it most certainly will be the last. Please, please do not say anything to anyone.

I should go and meet the other inmates. It is happy hour by the pool and I don't want to miss it. I snuck in a few duty free bottles of champagne. Only joking!

Love you
Anna xx

And then I write to Mark.

The touch of a hand that rolls down my spine and your breath on my neck
Hands moving over my body
A slight moan from my lips
I can feel myself giving in to your pleasurable touches.

Your mouth on my neck eagerly eating and taking in my flesh
I can feel you so hard against my back wanting me, wanting
*   you back.*
Slowly I turn to face you.
My tongue darts in your mouth, our lips lock into what seems
*   like an eternity*
Time stands still.
Our eyes search each other's soul, desire at breaking point
The moment is perfect
Desire, wanting, longing
We fall to the floor and my clothes slip off with such ease.
You take me slowly, gently then faster, slower
A whirlwind of sounds, touches, emotions
The flashing of the past, the future, the others, they are all
*   invisible nothing matters*
The moment is now and at that moment we are both free.
The purity of our love is flying
So high nobody can touch us
And this releases us both to a higher place
A world created in our minds that we both understand
A place that can't be described just lived.

Mark D'Arbanville

Seventy-nine

I wander the grounds. I see a girl sitting on her own on a bench at the end of the gardens. She is not reading or writing letters, just sitting, staring at the shadows of the blue mountains and there is on her face a look of ineffable sadness.

– Hi.

She looks up and her face creases into an uncertain smile.

– Anna, I say.

– Katya.

Katya is Polish, but lives in Paris. She is being treated for a drug addiction, she says. Her family are very wealthy and they can afford little indulgences like this, she says. This particular indulgence has lasted six months. Six months! Her English is very good and she has an appealing accent.

– What about you? she asks, and stares at the bandage on my wrist.

I try to hide it, keep my arm at my side.

– I lost my memory after a car accident.

– Is that why you tried to kill yourself? she says, pointing to the bandage.

– I didn't try to . . . this was . . . an accident.

I realise how lame it sounds.

Katya gives me a curious smile.

– Why do you want your memory back?

– I want to know who I am.

– And you think remembering will tell you that?

It was funny, that was what Mark had said.

Katya rubs her hands together like she is trying to remove a stain. She has scratches and cigarette burn scars up both her arms.

– Most people would love to erase their past. I would love to forget mine. Maybe you're lucky, Anna.

Maybe I am. So why don't I feel lucky at all?

Mark D'Arbanville

Eighty

The first four weeks pass quickly. Every day there are long sessions with Dr Francisco, her methods seem to revolve around certain medications combined with hypnotherapy. Dr Francisco thinks that my erratic behaviour and my memory loss are not just the result of the accident; that there is something else.

I look around at some of the other patients and I have to admit that Katya may be right; perhaps I am one of the lucky ones.

Dr Francisco is an attractive, dark haired woman, around my age. She wears tweed suits and spectacles but when she crosses her legs I notice she is wearing a garter belt under her skirt. And she wears Gaultier to work.

She flicks through pages and pages of handwritten and typed notes. Finally she sets the file aside and looks at me.

– Anna, your husband told us that you were seeing a therapist before the accident. Did you know that?

No, I didn't know that. Was anyone going to tell me?

– I asked him to send us his notes. I have been going through them. There is frequent reference to a man called Mark. Do you remember this man?

She looks at me over the top of her glasses. I nod my head.

– Tell me about him.

I take a deep breath.

– Anna kept all these emails they passed between each other . . . at the beginning they just . . .

– Not Anna. I. We're talking about you, not someone else.

– At the beginning I . . . *we* . . . just emailed each other. We tried to see who could write the cleverest emails. He made me laugh out loud. He called it the war on aphorisms, making fun of George Bush. There was such an amazing connection between us, emotionally and creatively, he made me feel good about myself and I think I did that to him as well.

– It sounds like the perfect relationship.

– The emails he sent and what I sent to him . . . the writing was exciting, dangerous. Then something changed. It was no longer about friendship, there were accusations and demands. Either I leave Paul or I stay with my husband and he could not still be my friend.

Dr Francisco looks at me over the top of her glasses and waits for me to speak. When I do not comment, she shrugs and says, go on, Anna.

– After that so much of the love and friendship evaporated. My responses became more and more guarded and unclear and confused. It was like a slow death in words. I told him I was not responsible . . .

– Are these memories, Anna, or what you read in the emails?

I feel the tears come.

– These are memories.

She smiles.

– Well, that's progress, at least.

Is it? I wonder. It doesn't feel like progress.

– I told him I was not responsible, but I absolutely felt like I was. And then his wife . . .

– She killed herself. It was all your fault, Anna. You're a murderer.

I stare at her, numb.

– That's what you've been telling yourself, isn't it?

– I am responsible.

– Well, you're not but I understand why you would think that.

She sighs.

– This relationship seems to have caused you a lot of distress and soul searching. Your doctor has written a clinical analysis. Do you want me to read it to you?

I shrug my shoulders. I feel utterly violated, raw to the very bone. An old wound opens, the suppuration oozing out.

Dr Francisco adjusts her glasses and reads:

Anna is a very intelligent woman in her mid thirties. From the outside she would be seen as a healthy and well adjusted woman. She is very adept at answering questions about herself and her inner life, and she can make it appear to the world that there is nothing wrong. She maintains that she has a wonderful family and good friends. She convinces herself and others that she is content, even very happy, but closer probing reveals contradictions and inconsistencies that do not gel with the picture she portrays.

Anna is highly skilled at debate. In direct confrontation she is very adept at protecting her points of view and in making even the most irrational behaviour appear consistent.

But on the few occasions that she allows her guard to drop, another Anna emerges. She is repelled by older men being near her or around her and is physically repulsed at being touched. She cannot explain why this should be so. I suspected very early in our program that she was a victim of some type of abuse, either mental or physical or both. As soon as we touched on this subject she would find a way to divert the discussion to something else.

Anna has been in an extramarital affair for the last few years. This man is integral to her healing but is also symbolic of her symptoms. She wanted this man as her special friendship, something that no one would know about or could touch or violate.

She wanted this man to care for and nurture her. She was desperate for this, but at the same time the most integral thing for her was to have a man to love her, a real friend who would be there for her, and not want anything in return. The contradictions in this are self evident.

When the man's wife committed suicide Anna went back to somewhere locked within her own mind.

There is no doubt she still finds great inspiration, challenge and joy from the friendship. But most importantly, he was

Mark D'Arbanville

someone she did not have to care for. This was crucial and raises many interesting questions about the nature of her other relationships, especially that of her marriage.

This need derives from a childhood violation of trust. Her distrust of men is intense. She is conflicted over the affair and the adultery. In her conversations she focuses a great deal on the undeniable bonds made on a creative and emotional level, while trying to ignore the evidently overwhelming sexual attraction, which she prefers not to examine in any depth.

I could feel the doctor's kind eyes on me.

– Is that how you see yourself, Anna?

I shrug my shoulders. I cannot look at her.

– All my life I've wanted to be self sufficient. I've never wanted to rely on anyone. Not for money, not for love. If I could do that, then I'd always be in control, and I could leave if I wanted.

– There's an irony there, Anna, isn't there?

– An irony?

– Because you don't feel as if you could ever leave your husband. You aren't really acting out of choice. Where is your independence?

I want to rip out her throat. How dare she speak to me that way.

– So this self sufficiency is an illusion?

– I didn't want to be like my mum. She has to stay. She has no choice.

– What is your mother like, Anna?

– She is the most beautiful soul I have ever known.

– You remember this?

– I know it. In my heart.

– What happens if you take a risk, Anna?

– You lose. You always lose. You get hurt and you lose. I put myself at risk once and I promised myself I'd never do it again, not ever.

– When did you last put yourself at risk, Anna?

I feel my heart lurch. I don't answer.

Dr Francisco sips water from a plastic bottle and refers to her notes. The silence goes on for a long time.

– This other man. Mark. He's a risk. He's unpredictable. How could you trust him, Anna? How could he trust you?

– I don't know.

– You must have worried about falling in love with him. If you fall in love, you lose control.

I am tired of people analysing me, asking me questions, wanting to know why I do what I do. I can't think anymore. I don't want to answer any more questions.

– I don't know, I repeat.

– That's okay, Anna. That is probably enough for now. We can talk again tomorrow.

I hurry out of her office. When I get back outside I sit on a bench in the garden, put my head in my hands and cry.

Mark D'Arbanville

Eighty-one

Live with one another

How do you stop the thoughts, the flashes of colour, happiness and pain?
One moment you are up flying amongst the clouds and the next you are ploughed into the earth with such feelings of absolute shame.
Is this the life you wanted?
Is this the life you planned?
I don't know, but I am still here and I am trying, just trying to understand.

My heart is sometimes pure and at other times as dark as one can be, but I am hiding, deep inside, hiding a big part of me.

But why they ask, you can have everything you want?
I cry out in pain they just don't fucking understand it is buried so deep they won't understand.

I wish it showed up as bruises because this is what you could show,
see I have lots, and you can put them out to show,
but you can't because the scars are hidden they just cannot see, they
    want to,
but can't imagine, the same pain under me.

Sometimes I am even comforted by this pain inside of me –
I try and be thankful for everything and positive to the bone,
because if you have seen the other side you don't ever want to
    return.
I just have the memories the flickering the light
The intense darkness my eyes closed so tight,
it will be finished soon and they will let me get up this time.

As I look into the mirror I see two of me if I hold my breath tight
    the other one floats past me
I stare hard, transfixed and I wonder, how two of me can be so
    different from one another –
sometimes they blend and other times they go so far away from one
    another,
but as I look into the mirror as they float back to one it's just me
    and we have to live with each other.

Mark D'Arbanville

Eighty-two

I have some letters with me from Paul. They were in the packing box at the back of my closet, the one with my diary and my old sports trophies. They were in a shoe box. Those days before email.

Reading through the letters I sent him I see a very insecure Anna, desperate for attention, desperate for him to love her and build her esteem, desperate for someone who would stop her hating herself.

His letters back must have been what my spirit needed; he said he missed me and couldn't wait to get back to me. Yet there is an undercurrent of restlessness too. He was overseas, travelling, and I had wanted to go and visit him, I had already bought my air ticket and I was bursting to tell him so I wrote and told him what I had done and he had written back and told me not to come.

This is a painful letter to read. I can see in my own answer to his rejection the scrawled and bitter words from an angry and wounded heart. But by the end of the letter the anger had turned full circle: I finished by telling him I loved him, and that I understood.

This is me. This is the Anna I had forgotten.

But then there was this, from after I met Mark, from when I was the one in control:

Dearest Anna,

I know I have made so many mistakes but I love you, I love you too much, and it scares me. You seem to have a hold over me and I don't like it and I think I take this out on you sometimes. You are just too much. It is hard for me to write this. I feel like I have let you down in so many ways and your constant need for me to tell you that you are okay gets to me, but it wasn't my intention to hurt you. It is very hard for me to put into words how I feel. I am back next week and I can't wait to see you. Let's go away up the coast like we used to. You always loved that and we can talk and laugh.

Paul x

A postcard:

You are amazing Anna the weekend was wonderful I have never laughed so much in ages I think I have fallen in love with you all over again XX Paul

It is clear from the letters that Paul is quite cerebral in many ways. Put together with someone who needed safety and calm, he was the perfect fit; intellectually challenging, supportive but not suffocating.

I did not want anyone who would get too close to me.

He loved in a cerebral rather than a physical way. There was a lot of emotional and physical distance and it seemed the Anna I had been had liked that. She liked to nurture and I was the nurturer in the relationship, but that also made me independent. I was the one in control of just how much distance there was.

I was the one in control. I am the one in control.

Katya appears and sits down on the seat next to me. She is pale and her eyes are red rimmed from crying.

– What's wrong, Katya?

She has her journal cradled in her arms. There are two fresh burn marks on the insides of her arms, and another two are weeping yellowish fluid. She is breathing too fast.

– I got a letter today.

– Bad news?

She shrugs.

– It was from my uncle.

– You're close to your uncle?

She gives me a look of contempt that I cannot fathom.

– What is it, Katya?

– There's a lot I never told you.

Even though I have asked the question, I am not ready for this. I don't want her pain. I am here for mine, I don't want this burden. All my instincts warn me what she is about to say. I feel as if I am going to be sick. Faces, men's faces, rush at me. It is hard to breathe.

– My family didn't send me here just because of the drugs.

– Why then?

– I tried to kill my uncle with a knife.

I want to get up and run. But I cannot move. I sit there as Katya presses the screwed-up pages into my hands and tells me to read the letter her uncle has sent; how can he say such things, she sobs, like it never happened, as if she was making the whole thing up?

– Or maybe that was it, perhaps it never happened, perhaps I did make it up, Anna. I am just a bad girl with stories, and I make them all up!

– What happened, Katya?

As if I don't know. As if I can't guess.

Katya is rocking back and forward with her legs crossed underneath her. Twenty-three years old and she looks like a child. Her face looks off into the distance as if she is staring at a horror movie on a theatre screen.

I cannot bear to touch her. I want to run back to my room, look at the mountains, write a letter to Paul. Get back in control. Not feel. But I sit there. I tell Katya she can talk to me. As the shadows lengthen across the garden and the afternoon grows chill, she tells me her story.

She was twelve years old the first time.

But you know, he was her favourite uncle. Her father was always at work and her uncle was the one who took her to the zoo and to the movies and he was always such fun. He was the first hero she ever had. She loved him. She loved him so much, so she must have imagined it all.

– I make things up in my head all the time, Katya says.

He said it never happened, he said he never did it, and he

Mark D'Arbanville

said if she ever told anyone he would go to prison and, anyway, everyone would blame her, her parents would divorce, is that what she wanted? Only it never happened again and again and each time he started crying and begging her not to tell and then he'd scream at her that it was her fault and he would have to go away because she was such a bad girl, and she didn't want him to go away, she didn't want everyone to be unhappy because of her, it was never going to happen again, he promised, let's pretend this never happened, and they could do that because it would never ever happen again. Until the next time he took her to the zoo and then back to his house for milk and cookies and he sat her on his lap and put his hand right up here on her leg.

And Katya shows me her inner thigh where she has scratched and scratched with scissors so that it is a patchwork of crusted scars.

And afterwards he cried again and then next day he came to the house and brought her a special treat, gelato, and he was laughing and joking and it was like it never happened and that was how she wanted it to be, like it never happened.

I jump to my feet. I cannot listen to any more. *There are hands around my throat, and something hits me hard over the back of the head and there is something in my mouth and I cannot breathe.*

I run to the bushes and I am physically sick.

Katya is bending over me, stroking my hair and telling me everything will be all right.

– Have you told the doctors about this, Katya?

– No, Anna, I can't, no one knows, nobody. You mustn't

say anything to anyone. He'll go to prison. I'm just a dirty liar! Maybe it never happened.

– Katya, your legs . . .

– *You can't say anything to anyone. None of the doctors know – do you hear me? You have to promise me!*

She hugs me and I hold her, I hold her until it starts to get too dark and cold to be outside and we can no longer see the mountains.

There is a time before the end of innocence, a time when we do not blame ourselves for things that have been done to us, a time when trust is not betrayed and our fledgling girl-hood dreams of sex are not broken by choking cloths and rough men's hands, a time when we are not always afraid.

But Katya and I, we do not know when that time is. We cannot remember. We just want to be left alone.

And in a way, we both have been and we both are.

Mark D'Arbanville

Eighty-three

I go back to my room, I lie on the bed and stare at the ceiling. I cannot move. A feeling of absolute dread paralyses me. I am covered in sweat like cold grease. I am shivering with cold.

I feel sick. I had longed for memories, any memory, to come back but not this. Not memories of men stuffing rags in my mouth. Not memories of men leering at me, faces like torturers, doing things to me I cannot see. I twitch and jerk on the bed and suddenly I am on my feet and running. I have to get away.

Who were they? Who were those men? What am I remembering?

I run into the toilet and I retch again. There is sweat dripping off me, I can smell it, sour and pungent, and I retch so hard that it hurts my throat.

I can't fucking breathe!

I rinse my mouth out in the sink and when I look at myself

in the mirror there is a hand around my throat squeezing and *if you ever tell anyone about this I will kill you, do you understand?*

I retch again into the sink, and when I look up I see I have vomited so hard it has made my nose bleed.

I scream and scream and scream and when the nurses find me I am lying on the cold tiled floor and there is blood everywhere and I am sitting there in the corner under the washbasins and I have written on the glass mirrors in reverse writing:

I KILLED HER.

I cannot move I must not move if I move they will hurt me I will concentrate on the wall if I just think about the wall the men cannot get back inside my head and hurt me anymore, they have pinned my wrists but if I just concentrate on the wall and they are hurting me but if I just concentrate on the wall and I cannot breathe and they are going to kill me but if I just concentrate on the wall eventually I will start to float and I can be up here in the air, here where I am alone and I am floating and it is safe and I can watch the nurses pressing the alarm and calling for the doctors and I am alone I am alone I am alone.

Mark D'Arbanville

Eighty-four

He watches him sometimes and wonders how easy it is to be young. They sit in companionable silence in the coffee shop, across the road from the cinema. Just sixteen years old and almost as tall as his father. When did that happen?

– So. You okay?

– I'm okay, Mark lies.

Mark waits. There is something on David's mind.

– I don't get it.

– What don't you get?

– Why you're still here. Why you aren't with her.

– She doesn't want me with her, that's why.

His coffee is cold and nearly gone but he pours another sugar in it and stirs it with his spoon. Then he pushes the cup away.

– It's all right, he says. You can talk about it if you want.

Strange, Mark thinks. My son wants to be my counsellor now. Well, why not? Another shin down off that pedestal.

– I mean, what is it? Was she just playing you off the break?

Playing me off the break, Mark thinks. What, he's had two girlfriends, three? How does he know about playing off the break?

– I don't know. I think she was never going to go with me. It seems to me that when the result's a foregone conclusion, does it matter what you make the reason to be?

David thinks about this. Shrunk down to size, Mark feels like a fool. He imagines his son will have to wait a lifetime to understand him, if then.

– I'm sorry, Mark says. It's hard to talk about this with you.

– Mum loved you to death, David says, and his son's jagged choice of words would be admirable in another situation.

– Look, I loved your mum, she was a brilliant mother –

– You don't have to preface everything you say about her by telling me how great she was. It's okay.

– But it's true.

– I want to know what you felt, not what you think.

Mark looks desperately around the coffee shop. What's a soy latte when you need a stiff drink?

So many things that David could not understand, that many people might not understand. Until he met Anna he thought it was just him, that he was crazy.

When you think your dreams cannot exist, you berate yourself for being foolish and a dreamer, try to put the longing to one side, accept what you have, what you have always had. Remember to be grateful that you are loved in a world of fire and ice.

And then one day you stumble across what you didn't

think could be. It's possible, you think. So what are you going to do, keep on compromising? Or do you have a shot at it?

– The person you fall in love with when you're twenty, they're not the same when you're forty, and neither are you.

– But she loved you.

Mark thinks about her journals. Did she really? Or did she just not want to lose him, because she was terrified of change? Two different things.

– We loved each other, David. But this wasn't about love. This was about . . .

What? What was it about? Their marriage survived if they did not spend too much time together. Something fundamental was missing, yet they were afraid to part.

– One day maybe you'll understand.

And Mark thinks, *one day maybe I will.*

He can see by his son's face that he doesn't really understand. Why should he? He's barely sixteen, for Christ's sake. He thinks he will always feel the way he does right now.

David is quiet for a long time. Mark wonders what he's thinking.

– Anna said to me over and over, if it wasn't for her, I would still be married. Like keeping the status quo is the most important thing in the world. Maybe she was right, maybe I would have still been married. But you know what? Nothing would be different. Maybe another five years, and she would have done the same thing, and I'd be five years older and five years lonelier.

David shrugs and scratches his head.

– You're thinking, yes, but at least I'd still have had my mother for a few more years.

– No, Dad. I would never have wanted you to pretend just for me. That's bullshit. At least now you're being fucking real.

Our eyes meet. He has honoured me with the F word, is talking to me like he talks the rest of the time. He's not pretending either.

– You know, David, if security ever becomes my bottom line, I don't think I could look in the mirror again and like what I see.

Mark leans forward and puts his hand on his son's arm.

– We've never had that father and son talk, but I want to say this to you, and I know perhaps it's presumptuous, seeing what's happened to me these last three years, but I'll say it anyway. Whatever you do, never be afraid to take risks. All I know is God didn't put us here on this earth to cling like oysters on a rock.

– You took a risk. Look what happened. You lost her. You lost both of them.

– I didn't lose anything. I didn't want what I had with your mum, and I never had anything with Anna, not anything that was mine to lose at least. Besides, if I knew she was waiting for me, it wouldn't have been a risk, would it? I took a risk when I decided to write for a living. Everyone thought I was crazy. But I risked it, and I never regretted it. That risk transformed my life.

There are tears in my son's eyes.

– David?

– It's not you, he says.

– What is it?

– Every now and then, I catch myself being happy. It means I'm leaving her behind. Every day I leave her behind a little more. She's never going to see me do the good stuff, is she? She's not going to see me get my first job or be there when I get married, nothing. If I'm happy I forget what it was like when she died and I don't want to forget . . .

I hug him.

To heal, as to forgive, is a mountain to climb. Happiness can be betrayal, because to look to the future is to forget the past, and leave behind what lives there, the monsters as well as the beloved.

If he's happy again, he loses his mother forever. She will fade, and pain is all he has to keep the past alive, and unforgotten.

Eighty-five

I sit in Dr Francisco's office. They gave me sedatives to help me sleep. Now, I stare out of the doctor's window at the washed blue of the sky over the mountains, a cold crisp morning. The doctor smiles at me and flicks through the file on her desk. My life is a file. I am someone's case study. Only I am also me and I am alone.

I am glad my doctor is a woman. You can never trust a man.

I run a finger over the scar on my wrist. It is still a livid pink but soon it will fade and heal. But do wounds ever heal? You have to get the poison out first. They say a wound won't ever heal while there is still poison in it. You have to open it up and drain it and then you can let it close over.

– Do you know what retrograde amnesia is? she asks me.

– It's something you can write in your file. Something to dissect me, explain me, box me into shape.

– It's a form of memory loss caused by a traumatic accident.

Mark D'Arbanville

Usually it means the patient has no recall of recent memory before the accident. But in theory you should still have recall of your childhood, but you don't. It is intriguing. There is no known way to restore memories lost through retrograde amnesia, that is, loss through physical trauma. That is why you are here, we specialise in other forms of therapy, as you have witnessed for yourself, psychotherapy and hypnosis. Doctor Maddison even suggested that you might have deliberately prolonged the effects of the amnesia. That there is an emotional component to your memory loss. Do you think this might be true?

I do not answer her.

– Do you remember what happened last night, Anna?

There is a tight band around my chest. I want to retreat, hide in my secret garden, that other place inside where I can't see the men and I can't feel them hurt me.

In my secret garden there are bright flowers and a warm and yellow sun. Only in my other world do I truly love my life. I can't be judged and I can't be hurt. It is all my own creation, no one else can influence the moods, no one else has demands, or wishes, or points of view, just me.

I know most people would think I was crazy if they knew. But if they could escape to another place where they felt safe and able to cope with the real world, wouldn't they do it?

It is my refuge from the demons. They can't go there and they can't find me there.

– Anna?

I force myself on. I think it will help if I start to talk, but I will talk as if I am talking about someone else.

– Anna remembered something, I say.

– Remember, Anna is you. It's you who are remembering.

I shake my head.

– She doesn't want to remember this.

– What is it you don't want to remember?

– She doesn't want to see these things in her head anymore. She can't seem to get them out. She wants to remember the faces of the kind people who love her but she keeps seeing . . . these other faces.

– What faces?

– She doesn't know who they are. They want to hurt her.

– Is this something that really happened, Anna?

I look down. I am digging my fingernails into the scar on my wrist. I have made the scar bleed again.

– Anna, let's take this very slowly.

She sits in the seat next to me and puts her arms around me.

– Anna always thinks –

– Don't talk about Anna, she says softly. Tell me about you.

– . . . I have this feeling one minute of being with someone who I trust, who I love, and he is a great friend. We have fun and we are laughing and then suddenly there is someone else there as well . . . a cloth is put into my mouth that smells, it really smells, it is like it is in the room now. I can smell it, it makes me sick.

I push her away from me and jump to my feet. I start pacing around the room. What is happening to me? What am I remembering? Perhaps I really am crazy.

– Out of the corner of my eye I see this person I think

Mark D'Arbanville

I trust . . . I know him and he is standing there, but he isn't helping me. Why won't he help me? My hands are being tied behind me right here . . .

I point to where I have cut myself.

— It hurts, it really hurts, and then I start to kick and try to scream but nothing comes out. I am choking on the cloth they put in my mouth. I can't do anything, my hands are tied and I pass out but before I close my eyes I can see his face, it is cold and it is not a face I have ever seen before on him and it makes me sick!

— You know him, Anna?

I shake my head.

— But he's your friend?

— You can't trust him! You can't trust anyone! They say they're your friend and they just turn into something else. He should have helped me. *Why didn't he help me*?

— Come and sit down, Anna.

I cannot sit down. Perhaps I am just being crazy. Perhaps she doesn't believe me. Perhaps no one ever will.

— Doctor, I really don't know what this is. It feels so real, but I can't help thinking it is my mind playing tricks on me. Yesterday afternoon someone told me about a rape and it just seemed . . . I was always good at making up stories.

— Anna, what you are feeling is so detailed. The sense of smell, the fear, the foreboding. I would suggest this is genuine memory. Something that was locked away for years, somehow, but because of the trauma you suffered and losing your other memories . . . somehow it has cleared the way for this to surface at last.

The Naked Heart

– No, no, you're wrong, doctor, this is not me, this is not me, I am happy, I have a successful career, I have a family that loves me, a normal sex life, this can't be true and nobody has ever told me about this, wouldn't people have known?

Dr Francisco just sits there and smiles. I think about what I have just said and I know what she is thinking. How could anyone know? Why is it that no one ever knows?

What about Katya? Only her uncle knew what had happened.

– NOOOOOOO!

– Anna, it will be all right. Just sit down.

I want to smash something, anything. I want to get out of this room. I do not want this horrible past. I want to be happy, I want my family to be normal and happy, I want my marriage and my life to be happy, I want everyone to be happy. Then no one will know there is anything wrong. Then nothing will be wrong.

– Anna, please, sit down. If it is getting too much we can stop, but I would like to keep going if you can. I feel perhaps you have been harbouring this memory for a very long time and perhaps this is the piece of the puzzle that has blocked you from remembering anything else.

I slump into the chair. I feel repulsed and drained and dirty. I want to shower and wash and scrub my skin, get the dirt and the shame and the smell of those men off of me, get the smell off me forever.

And I hear myself saying, I remember him dressing me, combing my hair, fixing me up. He was my friend, he was supposed to be my friend. I never saw him again and I hate

Mark D'Arbanville

him and I miss him. What is wrong with me? How can I be sad about not seeing that monster again? I must be sick, crazy. If I feel like this it means I wanted it to happen.

– How many times did this happen, Anna?

I shake my head. I don't know.

I don't know.

Eighty-six

– I can't see you anymore, she says.

– What?

She is lying on the couch, in her pyjamas, watching television. Her apartment is shabby chic, clean surfaces, every carelessly thrown rug carefully arranged. It is exactly two weeks to the day after he first told her that he was falling in love with her. Nothing has gone right since.

– I can't be responsible for someone else's happiness.

Mark has heard all this before.

– I told you at the beginning I just wanted a friend. I'm no good at relationships.

– So that's it. Like that?

She won't even look at him. Her face is cold, someone else's.

– We can still be friends.

Well, what did you expect? he asks himself. You're still in love with another woman. Not that it would have made a scrap of difference.

Mark D'Arbanville

– This was never going to be forever. I told you that.

– So what are you going to do, Maddy?

– I get scared. I always get scared.

He gets up and picks up his car keys from the kitchen bench. He has had this conversation before.

– You know, about a week ago, I had my head on your lap, down by the river, that Sunday afternoon, and I almost told you I loved you.

– Why didn't you? he asks her.

She shakes her head, won't answer. He hesitates at the door.

– You wrote that Christmas card to me. You said I was the most amazing man you'd ever met and that you were so lucky.

– I am lucky, lucky to have you as a friend.

Oh for God's sake. He should know better than to argue. They are like trial attorneys, these women, they can argue out anything so that words become meaningless in the end.

– I thought about you this week. I was worried about you. That I'd hurt you. You're the last person I wanted to hurt.

– Oh, fuck off, Maddy.

But don't you deserve this? he asks himself. Have you been honest with her? Wasn't there something desperate in your loving of this woman, if that was what it was? If Anna had come back and fallen at your feet, what would have happened to Madeleine? How honest have you been, have you ever been, with any woman aside from her?

He picks up his cell phone with its secret bank of text messages and walks out of the door. He doesn't say goodbye and he doesn't look back.

The Naked Heart

Eighty-seven

There are no locked gates at the clinic. We are free to come and go as we please and so far I have not explored further than the gardens. So next morning Katya wakes me early and tells me we are going into town. We run out through the wrought iron gates like schoolgirls on the last day of school. We catch a tiny bus that looks as if it is a hundred years old.

The bus driver lets us off in the town square. There is a fair, and there are people everywhere, kids screaming and even an ancient barrel organ. My spirits lift.

Katya buys sugar candy for us both. We wander around the side shows and someone yells out to us: *Belle donne, viene qui! Hey, beautiful ladies, come over here!*

The idea is to throw a ball into a hole in the wall. It looks easy but it really isn't. We throw and miss and laugh and miss again and the Italian boys flirt and try to speak English and French and Katya tries to speak Italian, and we laugh some more.

Mark D'Arbanville

Afterwards we wander out of the town. On the outskirts there are sunflower fields and we lie down in one of the fields with our hands behind our heads and let the sun warm us. It is a clear, crisp sky.

– What happened yesterday, Anna? Katya asks, her voice deceptively mild. What did you say to the doctor about me?

– Katya, I didn't say anything, okay?

Her eyes are hooded.

– When I saw Doctor Francisco this morning, she kept asking me if there was something I wasn't telling her . . .

– I didn't say anything.

We lie there looking at the sky, blue sky. I don't want to float there in the sky anymore. I want to be a part of life. I want to be free of being free.

– If you did, you would have done me a favour.

I lie there, and I can feel this terrible panic. I know what she is going to say.

– How did it happen to you, Anna?

Suddenly I am suffocating out here on this beautiful blue day. I experience the familiar feeling of floating above my body. Suddenly I am looking down at a woman lying on her back in a sunflower field, her looking back at me, me looking down at her. Her eyes are haunted, her face pale.

I listen to her tell her story as if she is someone else, as if it is some terrible thing that has happened to someone else, in a foreign country, in a foreign war, a long way away.

For the first time I want to go back to her, but I can't while this terrible pain is still inside her. It is too dangerous.

– Great, Anna! Brilliant! That's three seconds off your best time! I can't wait for the District Championships. You're going to be my little star!

I look up at Shelley. I have beaten her again. She hates me.

It worries me until I see his face. I will do anything for him. He puts a hand on my back. It feels warm and safe.

– My little star! he repeats.

He isn't nearly as old as some of the other teachers. He has fair wavy hair, and he looks more like a surfer than anything. He flashes me a smile, a beautiful smile.

He puts the stopwatch in the pocket of his track top.

– Get your breath and we'll do some distance work.

Finally he turns to my friend.

– Good work, Shelley. You'll get there. And that is all he says.

Afterwards in the showers Shelley hardly says a word to me. As I get out of the shower she is staring at me and her face is spiteful.

– He loves you, she says.

– He does not! I say, but secretly I am pleased, I want him to love me.

As we leave I see him walking past the change block.

– Goodnight, girls, he says and waves. See you tomorrow night!

Shelley stops, watching his back. There is a look on her face I have never seen before.

– I bet he was here all that time, she says. I bet he was watching us in the showers.

Mr Hicks? I suddenly feel sick. I cannot believe she would even think such a thing. Sour grapes.

– Creep, she hisses.

Mark D'Arbanville

I do wonder why he is still hanging around, why he hasn't driven straight home. There has to be a good reason. Shelley just wants to make up a reason to hate him because I am better than her.

And next day, after school, Shelley doesn't come to training. Mr Hicks is waiting out there on the track for me. I always feel such a glow when he looks at me. No one at home has ever paid me attention like this.

— Shelley came to see me today, he says. She's been picked for the netball team and she wants to spend more time at practice. So it's just you and me for a while.

I try to look disappointed but secretly I'm pleased. I want all his attention, not just some of it.

He has the most brilliant blue eyes. He puts a hand on my shoulder.

— Are you willing to work really hard, Anna?

I nod eagerly. I will do anything for him.

— You could be the best, the very best. I've been coaching running for five years and I've never seen a girl with your talent. You might even run in the Olympics one day.

— Do you think?

— You'll have to do everything I say. You trust me?

Of course I trust him. He is my teacher, and he looks like a Greek god. I want to be great.

I nod and grin.

— Okay, let's start work on some sprints, he says.

I adore him. Is adore too strong a word? To adore. To idolise. To see someone as what they are not. I bask in the glow of him. He tells me I am wonderful and that I can be great one day. He is so energetic, so fresh and so beautiful. And I want to be loved.

He is my best friend.

My best friend Sue had left in year six, the year before. Her father had been transferred to PNG. I don't have anyone afterwards; I am always the third wheel, tacked on to other best friends, I have no one to talk to about stuff, but Mr Hicks has changed all that.

– Like a breath of fresh air, my mum says to me at the District Championships.

Even my dad likes him.

– You're going to be the next Dawn Fraser, he says, forgetting that Dawn Fraser is a swimmer and I have just taken first in the four hundred and eight hundred metres foot race.

– He's really made a difference to your running, Mum says.

And I get this look from Dad. He is proud of me. It is a look I yearn for, even today. That I ache for.

And after I get my medals Mr Hicks puts an arm around me and gives me this enormous hug, right there in front of Mum and Dad and the whole school. And on Monday everyone wants to be my friend. Mr Hicks is cool. He surfs and he drives a red Charger and he is cool. And because he coaches me and thinks I am the best, I am cool too.

I don't know that I was ever that good a runner. But he makes me think that I am, and I love him for that.

– You loved him, Katya says.

– He was my teacher.

– But you loved him. Your body was eleven, but you had a grown-up heart.

And I know she is talking about her uncle. But she is also talking about me and Mr Hicks.

Mark D'Arbanville

– Bit of hair loose, he says, and reaches down and adjusts my hair clip. He smells so good really close up. Ready to be a star? he says.

And I am, I am ready to be a star. I want to shine. I fly round the track, it is a cool summer night with the sun low over the city and I remember the sound of my breathing and hearing the hammering of my heart as I round the final bend and he is standing there at the finish line with his stopwatch in his hand. I can see he is excited and he is yelling at me, come on, Anna, come on, come on!

And I feel like I am flying, really flying, and as I cross the line he catches me with one arm and swings me around and kisses me on the mouth.

Then he sets me down on the ground.

– You beat your best time by nearly two seconds! he shouts at me.

But I don't really take it in. My lips are tingling from the kiss. I am sure it is an accident, that he had just meant to kiss me on the cheek, and he doesn't seem worried, he doesn't apologise or anything. And it did feel nice.

I have never even kissed another boy on the lips before. It is nice, but confusing. I like the feeling and I think I want him to do it again and that confuses me too. He is my teacher. He shouldn't kiss me on the lips. But it is so nice, and maybe if he thinks it is okay, then it is okay.

– It wasn't your fault, Katya says. I cannot look at her, but I hear the catch in her voice.

I don't say anything.

– Look, I remember rubbing myself against a table leg once.

I couldn't have been more than four years old. It felt so good. And then my mother walked in and I can still see the look on her face, like I was the devil. We were just kids, Anna. If it feels good we did it. It's like ice cream, and water slides. We didn't know there was anything different between sex feeling good and ice cream tasting good.

– I was eleven, Katya.

– And that made you still a kid.

– I should have done something. I should have stopped it.

– You were a kid!

– I wanted him to touch me!

Now Katya has me by the shoulders and she is shaking, she is hurting so much and her cheeks are wet and her eyes are crazy.

– Of course you did! Because it felt nice! But he's the one who knew the difference between eleven and twenty-one! Not you!

– *This is Joe, he says. Joe is a friend of mine. He's an athletics coach. He's trained Olympians. I asked him along to see you run.*

A part of me is really excited. I want him to like me and I want to impress him. For Mr Hicks. But the way he looks at me, there's something I don't like. I don't like someone else coming along on our sessions. I want Mr Hicks all to myself.

But the Olympics! And if he's a friend of Mr Hicks, then it must be all right.

– *Tony's been telling me what a talent you are, he says.*

Tony. He means Mr Hicks. I had never even considered he might have a first name.

Mark D'Arbanville

— Let's show him what you can do, Mr Hicks says, and he puts an arm around me and leads me to the track. He touches me a lot now. I like the feel of his arm around me, it feels so safe, but there's a part of me that thinks, well maybe not. He doesn't do this with any of the other kids at school. I wonder if it's all right. I wish I could talk to Mum or my dad or my sister about this.

— Show him what you can do, tiger, he says and I do, I run like I've never run in my life and as I get to the finish line, past my PB by a long way, he scoops me up in his arms and hugs me and I feel like the queen of the world.

And afterwards, when I am in the shower, I don't even hear them come in.

It's when I turn off the faucet and I see Mr Hicks standing there with Joe that my world stops and my world changes, not forever, but until today, when I tell Katya about it for the first time since it happened and I admit to another human being my deepest, wordless shame.

— It wasn't your fault! Katya is sobbing, clutching her knees to her chest. You were just a little girl! You were still in primary school!

— I asked for it, I tell her. That's what he told me and it's true.

— How could it be your fault?

— I liked him kissing me, I tell her, and I damn myself, I damn myself for all time.

He's my friend, my best friend. He thinks I'm a star.
Stop this. Save me. Please.

Before the world goes to black I look over at my best friend and his face is so cold. It is not Mr Hicks, it is someone else, it is a face I have never seen before and I will remember it always. I have learned that under every man there is a monster.

Katya is silent now. Her face is streaked with mascara and she is rocking back and forward on her haunches.

– Oh my God, she murmurs. Oh my God.

– He hated me, I whisper. He said he thought I was great and he pretended to like me and be my friend but deep down he just wanted to use me. He hated me, Katya, he really hated me.

– It wasn't your fault.

– No, I say, it wasn't my fault, but it was my fault, all of it. It had to be my fault because I loved him. I brought it on myself when I let him kiss me and tie my hair and pat me on the back. I wanted him to do it. I wanted all of it. And that's why it all went so wrong.

I lay on the floor, curled up into a ball, and he knelt down beside me stroking my hair. He was crying.

– I love you, he whispered. But you mustn't ever tell anyone about this. No one will ever understand. This has to be our secret.

I couldn't stop crying or shaking. My mind was just empty. I tried to think of something to say, something to think, but I couldn't. I just felt black and empty.

– If anyone ever finds out, it will be terrible. I'll have to go away. And they'll send you away too, from your family, from everyone. They'll say it was your fault.

Mark D'Arbanville

— You know you wanted this, it wasn't so bad, was it? he says, and he is still stroking my hair.

He starts to dress me.

— You mustn't ever tell anyone about this, he says. Never. Or something terrible will happen.

— We should have told, Katya says. It wasn't our fault.

I nod my head.

— They were great teachers, I tell her. They taught us how to lie and they taught us how to keep secrets and they taught us how to be ashamed.

After he has gone I shower, I try to wash it all off me. There are bruises on the inside of my legs and scratches where they pushed my legs apart. And when I look in the mirror I can't see me anymore, I just see them, and I know I have to stop crying. I have to not be me anymore or people will know something bad has happened and make me tell.

I get dressed and when I look back in the mirror I am not there. It is just an eleven year old girl and nothing bad has ever happened to her, she is fine, she is okay. No one is ever going to look inside and see. I can't let anything bad happen. I can't let everyone know what I made them do.

I watch myself walk home. No one is ever going to know. No one. I know he loves me. And one day I am going to make him love me the way he should. Like I always wanted him to.

Katya is holding me in her arms. I look up at the blue sky. I want to melt into it, be blue and silent and far away forever.

When I get home I run straight into the bathroom and lock the door. I rip my clothes off and I try to shove them down the toilet. I am jamming the toilet brush down the toilet, poking it harder and harder and harder. I feel so out of control. I try to flush the toilet but it is jammed now. I lift the cistern lid and drop it on my foot but I don't feel anything.

— Anna, honey, are you okay? What was that noise?

It's Mum, rapping on the door. I can't answer. Snot all over my face from crying and my throat feels like it has closed over. Okay, Anna, you have to get control of yourself. Switch.

What did he say to me? It never happened, did it, Anna? They won't believe you.

— I'm fine, Mum, I'll be out in a minute.

— Did something happen at school?

— I just had a fight at school. I'm okay. Go away.

I hear myself screaming at her, shouting just like Dad. I sound just like Dad.

The toilet is a mess. I am going to be in so much trouble again. I slide down the wall. I want to flush myself away, away, away. I look at the inside of my legs and wrists and there're bruises every-where. I will have to think up a reason for that — I guess that won't be too hard.

I jump in the shower. I don't have the energy to stand so I sit there on the floor watching the water drop down my body and I work out my plan. I will not run again. I will do something to my foot so I can't, then everyone will feel sorry for me and I will be okay.

I'll tell Mum I had a fight with Mr Hicks, tell her he said I'm not good enough. I will be very convincing. Already I'm feeling better — it never happened, we just had a fight and, anyway, who wants to

Mark D'Arbanville

hang around old teachers when I can be playing with my friends?

I will never be alone with another old man again NEVER I will never let any man touch my hair my face my skin NEVER I hate old MEN they should not be allowed to be near girls they just are disgusting they are horrible and vile you cannot trust them, they always tell you what to do, I will never let anyone any MAN tell me what to do, I will NEVER be alone with a man again and even if I am I won't be there, they will never have my full attention as I will always have something just for me I will never let all my secrets out NEVER.

NEVER.

I get out of the shower and grab my towel. I fish my clothes out of the toilet and throw them out the window. I'll get them later and bury them in the garden or throw them in the bushes in the park. I'll tell Mum they were stolen. Nothing happened today, nothing.

NOTHING.

Katya's arms are holding me tight. We are alone here, two hurt women in a world of men. I feel dirty, I feel disgusted with myself, with life, with God, with men, with everything. I just want to run back to my room and shower, wash it all off down the drain, everything.

I am tearing at my legs with my nails. I just want to scrub and scrub. There is slimy stuff inside my legs and I just want to get it off, get it off me.

But Katya holds me tightly in her arms.

— Oh, Anna, she murmurs. What are we going to do?

— It's all my fault, Katya, I tell her. It's because I wanted him to kiss me.

I know the truth now, what was hidden from me and what was hidden from that other Anna most of her life. I had been raped, betrayed, brutalised, had smelt death and sex before my first kiss. I wonder if that rope around my wrists will cut into my skin forever.

By the time I get back to the clinic all I want to do is hide in my room and never come out. I slam the door and curl up on the floor, gasping for air. Will my mind ever rest? Will I spend the rest of my life burdened with these nightmare dreams? Even when I close my eyes, they are there. Will I ever get away?

There is a garden shed at home. There is a rake standing against the wall. I lay it down on the floor of the shed and take off my shoe and my sock. And then I stamp down on it.

Two of the prongs go through the sole of my foot and I see the metal tips through the skin. There is blood everywhere. I scream and scream but it doesn't hurt that much. It is strange. There is no feeling in my body, not anywhere.

Everyone thinks it's an accident. And I never go to running practice again.

Next day I go to school on crutches. Everyone is sad for me because now I can't run in the state championships. Mr Hicks thought I would win.

And I see him in the corridor and I wait for him to come up and ask me about my foot. But he doesn't even look at me. I lean on the crutches and I can feel the throbbing pain in my right foot but the real ache is inside, deep in me. I have lost my best friend and it is all because I wanted to kiss him and because I let him play with my hair.

Mark D'Arbanville

I never see him again. He left the school and he didn't even say goodbye. I had ruined everything.

He was my very best friend and I am so sad that I will never ever see him again. Another part of me says, but he was a monster, what kind of sick and crazy person is in love with a monster? I must have wanted it. He must have been right. I must have.

They take me to all kinds of doctors, but it's easy to fool them, even when you're a kid. It's easy to fool people. You just have to find out what it is they want to hear.

I don't tell anyone, not anyone, what happened. After a while I don't even tell myself, I even think it never really happened. I didn't want it to happen, so it didn't. I can think about something else, I can make things go away, I don't have to feel. If you go away in your head, then no one can ever hurt you, they can't find you there.

The marks on my wrists are an ugly purple. I find a pair of scissors in the bathroom cupboard and start to slash at the bruises. It feels good and it stops me thinking about what has happened. This way Mr Hicks didn't do it.

I did.

There are stories, whispers, about Mr Hicks and another girl in year six, a girl called Sarah. There is an odd sense of betrayal, he was doing it to another girl while he was doing it to me.

I find her one day sitting under a tree in the school yard, eating her lunch on her own. I hardly know her. She is just this quiet kid with long dark hair and she looks a little bit like me, I suppose. And I am still on my crutches. I am breathing hard, I don't know where the anger is coming from, from a deep well, a big black well inside me that goes on and on forever.

— You did this! I scream at her. You disgusting little witch!

She goes white. She just stares at me.

— You made him leave the school! Everyone knows about you and him! Everybody hates you! Everybody!

There are fat tears rolling down her face but she doesn't cry. It is like she is numb.

— He didn't love you! He was my friend! And he had to leave because of you!

Her eyes are the saddest eyes I have ever seen. She sits there with these big tears rolling down her cheeks while I scream at her and the worst of it is I know how she feels. But inside I just feel cold. And she never comes to school again, not the next day, not ever. Later someone says she has had a nervous breakdown.

She looked so much like me. Even when I was screaming at her, I thought: she looks just like me.

That night I lie in bed, and I am drained and exhausted and terrified that I will fall asleep. I am scared of what I dream. I know what I will do. I will make up stories about all the other patients in the clinic, good stories, funny stories. I will invent a new life for myself and that is the world I will live in, a looking glass world where I can escape the demons that are coming in the dark behind my eyes. I see myself in my mind's eye, a child with her face buried in a favourite picture book, humming a nursery rhyme as loud as she can, to shut out the noises of the monsters throwing themselves at her bedroom window . . .

When I wake up next morning there are scratch marks on my wrists and the insides of my thighs. There is sweat on my stomach and my head is trapped in a vice.

I want to live, really live again, and not be afraid anymore. I want to be free.

Mark D'Arbanville

Eighty-eight

– **You broke up with Madeleine,** Jen says as soon as Mark walks in.

She is sitting at the table they share in her office, reading the draft of his script. A mist of rain falls in the garden, the snails eat her plants, the crows shiver on the wall – a grey, amorphous and suffocating world that clings damp and chill to the eaves and the blackberry bushes.

– Christ, you look like shit.

– Thanks. Coffee on?

– Help yourself.

He sits down and goes through the script, his mind far away, but he does a good impression of a fully functioning human being, offering suggestions with the script, the dialogue, plot points. Like he gives a fuck.

– You need closure, she says.

He stares at her across the table.

– How can you love someone else when you're waiting to see if she'll still love you?

– Well, I do my best.

– It's just so obvious. It's like a black cloud hanging over your head.

– Look, I know she's not coming back to me. But it's not something you get over. Not when it's like this.

The coffee is lukewarm and bitter. He pushes the cup away. He doesn't want it, doesn't need it. It's just something to do with his hands. Keeping busy. His whole life now is just about keeping busy.

– But you don't know, do you?

– No, you're right, I don't know. For once you're right, Jen, you're so fucking right. I need closure. I need the door to slam shut or open wide. And it's not going to happen. If she's a cold, calculating, manipulative bitch then I've just done my money. I'm dead in the water. I don't think she is.

– You're history, boy.

– You see, I know what's she going to do. She's going to leave me and tell me she is going to love me forever. And that will leave me totally fucked. Because her love will be there and she won't be. It's the worst possible thing she could do, but that is what she will do. I know her well enough by now.

– Then why do you stay?

– Because I don't want to be one of those countless people you see wandering around, drifting in and out of relationships pretending they're there and all the time they're wondering why the one love of their life never worked out. So give me a platitude, Jen. Give me common sense and logic. None of it works.

He opens his notebook, stares at the last note he made on

Mark D'Arbanville

the script. *What is her motivation?* But life is not a script or a film, and its Black Moments can sometimes go on forever and sometimes people don't really understand their motivations and sometimes there is not a Hollywood ending.

– Let's do the script, he says, and for once Jen does not have a smart answer, or any answer at all.

Eighty-nine

There are letters from Paul and from Mark.

Here is my life, here in my hands. Both men wanting me, neither man getting all of me. Both men lied to and deceived by me. Both loved and inspired by me. Both hated me at times. Both apparently still in love with me.

And here are the three women I have become. The Anna Mark loved, the Anna Paul loved and the Anna I see in the mirror, the Anna I am right now.

I rip open Paul's letter.

Dear Anna,

Sweetheart, how are you? I miss you so very, very much. God, the house is so big with you not in here. I still talk to you every day and I have left all your clothes everywhere, like the day you left. I keep expecting you to walk in. I see you everywhere.

Even if you can't remember anything, Anna, that is okay, we can start again, build new memories and the family we talked about, okay?

I miss you desperately.

Love always
Paul

I open Mark's letter.

Dear Anna,

I hope the treatment is going well and you are finding your answers. I don't know what to say; I am going away for a while, to LA. I have picked up some work on a TV series there. It might be the change I need.

There have been so many words. Now there are not enough.

Mark

Ninety

Anger.

My heart starts to race. I want to write Paul and Mark a letter but instead I just kick and scream. They both want something I can't give, perhaps I never gave, perhaps because I don't want to fucking well give it!

Fuck them all.

My father. Who I have lived in fear of my whole life. And me, all of us, playing happy families for him.

Fuck my memories, my past. My teacher. What kind of man was he? What kind of men can do something like that to a little girl? What is going on in their heart, in their soul? What legacy did they leave me? How was I supposed to get on with a life after they did what they did?

I hope they rot in hell.

Why the hell did those doctors save me?

I look at Paul's letter. *We can start again, build new memories and the family we talked about, okay?* What did he do with our

Mark D'Arbanville

marriage? Why was I so fucking lonely? Why was I able to have an affair for three years without any questions asked? How the fuck could that happen if he loved me so much, like he says?

Why do I always get the feeling that I am less than him? Why does everyone else think he is so fucking perfect? If he is like they say, why did I have an affair with someone else? Am I some bitch who can never be satisfied with just one man?

Yes, he seems to love me a lot now, but was it always like that? Mark says it wasn't. Can I believe him? It seems to fit, but without my memory how will I ever know?

Paul travels all the time for work. Why did he never ask me to go with him? Why didn't we ever go to Paris before? Why didn't he ever surprise me before? Why did his mother decide we would have a baby? Was he always controlled by his mother?

Why does he bottle up so much inside of him and never let me know what he is thinking. Why is it always about me? In the whole time I have been home he has hardly ever expressed how he really feels, it is always about me. Was he always like that? Was he always so distant?

Why didn't he romance me, love me like he should, love me openly and wonderfully, because if he had I wouldn't have had an affair and Mark would still be with his wife.

Mark. He seems to love a version of Anna, he loves to tell me how that Anna should be, some other Anna he has made up inside his stupid head, always telling me what I should do, what I should think. Well fuck him. Did I ever tell him what he should be? Like he's Mister Perfect? He dragged me into that shit with his wife and son – why is it always about me, the woman who can't decide and who is breaking his god-damn glass heart?

I want to hit him, strangle him, make him stop talking. This constant mental torture, always analysing my emotions, who or what I was. He sucks the life out of me, I can't breathe around him.

So he can't love anyone else. Well he was doing a good job of it that night in the club.

Sometimes I really hate him for coming into my life and bringing with it a tidal wave of love and pain plus a whole entire family. I guess I loved it in the beginning, being pro-tected by him, getting his advice but having to make my own choices. Sometimes I feel as though he thinks we are identical and he can give me a detour around my pain. I don't think it works like that. We are similar in so many ways, but we are not carbon copies. This constant pressure from him to be able to react as he does is confronting. Perhaps I get cynical and I don't trust what he is saying is good for me anymore, it is just good for him. I don't want someone to tell me who I should be, I want to move towards the real me, and only I can decide what that is. Otherwise I am just another version of what society or Mark wants and needs me to be.

I take the pillow and throw it against the wall, then pum-mel my fists into it. It is Mark's head. Fuck him, fuck him, FUCK HIM! What did I ever see in him? He wants to con-trol everything I do, always ranting on about what I did, and being real. Get over it, you bastard, I'm not your project, your fucking thesis, your yes-girl no-girl.

Mark D'Arbanville

He can show me as many old text messages as he wants, he can say I deny my feelings and live in my head, blah, blah, blah, but at the end of the day he is just trying to control me, like every other fucking man in my life, and something inside me tells me I don't want to be controlled. Perhaps that's my father's curse – I don't want to end up like my mother.

I have shredded the pillow. Well, Paul's controlling fucking mother can pay for that. It was good therapy.

I sort through my bag to find some tissues and I come across two photographs, one of my husband, the other my crazy lover who hates me. Mark's picture was taken in Paris, I recognise the Notre Dame in the background. I should understand. I know I love him, I always feel that energy, that spark when I am with him. But since I woke from the coma all I have seen is a shell of a man telling me I am a fucking neurotic mess who has fucked up his life.

I think I have remembered enough. I have done with the past.

Ninety-one

No one knows I am coming home. I don't want a big
scene at the airport. I know what I have to do, and I want only
to get it done.

I take a cab from Heathrow to home. Paul is at work.
I wander around the rooms, stare at the photographs and the
books, stare at our wedding photograph. God, I had loved
Paul so much. He was all I ever wanted. I know that this is not
enough for me now. I have changed, and our lives have
changed forever. When you feel the dark angel breathe on
your face, and you remember that you are not going to live
forever, you cannot come back to life the same as you were
when you nearly left it. You want more, you demand more,
you feel you deserve more.

I hear a key turn in the lock. Paul is home.

I take a deep breath.

His face is transformed in a moment.

– Anna! My God, Anna!

Mark D'Arbanville

He wraps me up in his arms. For once I do not mind. It feels so good to have his arms around me, I don't want this moment to end, I want the clock to freeze. For now he is happy. In a few minutes I know I will change all that.

I feel the tears come. This will be the hardest thing I will ever have to do in my whole life.

– Anna, he is saying, it's okay, you are home now, everything is going to be okay. I have missed you so much!

I know these few words are all it will take to weaken my resolve. I can make him happy, or I can bring him to utter despair. I want him to be happy. I don't want to hurt anyone. Until this moment, I have always saved him, have always chosen to save everyone, before I saved myself.

I hesitate. Can I do this? Do I want to do this? But it is too late, the words are already pouring out of me. I push him away.

– Paul, sit down, please. I have to tell you something.

His smile vanishes. He knows what is coming.

– There is something I have to tell you. Before the accident, I was having an affair with another man. I was having an affair for nearly three years.

The look on his face makes me feel physically sick. But I am going to do this. I promised myself.

– I saw him again soon after I left the hospital, and I slept with him.

Paul sits there and doesn't move. His face is immobile. A tear tracks down his cheek but he doesn't say anything. There is a pain in my stomach and I cannot stand up anymore. I sit down on the edge of the lounge. This is even worse than I imagined. I want this to be over. I want to be true and honest. I don't want to have secrets anymore. There have been too many secrets and I want them banished, gone. I kneel down in front of him and put my head in his lap. He is sobbing like a child. This is unbearable, unbearable.

– Sweetheart, I understand if you never want to see me again. What I did was unforgivable. I should never have seen him again after the accident. I am so sorry.

– I . . . I understand. I know I can be . . . a little distant sometimes. You are a passionate woman . . . that is who I fell in love with and I did not let you know how much I so desperately love and need you.

How much heartache can one human being inflict on another? The worst of it is that I loved him, in my way. No one can ever understand that. He was my friend and my life's companion. I knew him better than I knew another living soul in the whole world. He had been my life. How will I wake up in the morning and not find him there? But I did not love him in the way I should, in a way that was enough for me as a woman. I just can't make it work, not now, not anymore.

I take his face in my hands. Oh God. If I close my eyes, I can do this, I can't look at his face.

– Paul, I am going away. I am going to make a new start somewhere else. I am going to try to write and develop some scripts. Make a new life. I think it will be for the best in the end.

– Anna, please don't leave me again, we can make this work. I don't care about the affair, we can leave it in the past, we can make it.

Mark D'Arbanville

His desperation overwhelms me. I feel myself weaken. But for once I have to do something for me, for my pain, not his, not Mark's, not my family's.

– It's over, sweetheart. You know that. I am going to pack a few things and then I am leaving.

I have already called Sally, and I will stay with her for a few days until I can organise flights and somewhere to live. I have asked Sally not to tell anyone I am there. I need to summon my strength to do this.

I walk out of the room. I just cannot stand to see the hurt I have caused. All my life I have tried to avoid causing pain. But you can't avoid it, in the end.

– Where are you going? How will I contact you? The desperation in his voice has changed to anger.

– You can't contact me, I say, my face turned the other way.

– What the hell are you doing, Anna? You cannot do this, please!

He stands up and grabs me by the arm.

– Don't do this! What about your family, your friends? If you don't care about me, what about them?

– Paul, I love them all, and I do care about you. But I need to do this for me. I am no good for anyone until I'm good for me.

He runs out, slamming the door behind him. I follow. He jumps into his car, sobbing, his face twisted in grief. God, what have I done to this man?

– Paul!

The door is locked. I beat with my fist on the driver's side window. But he reverses wildly out of the driveway, scrapes the passenger door on the gatepost, almost hits a motorcyclist in the street. He drives off, too fast.

I run inside and fetch my mobile phone, ring his car phone on my speed dial. It is switched off. I ring constantly for an hour. Finally he picks up.

– Paul, thank God. Where are you, baby?

His voice sounds flat, lifeless.

– I'm okay. I'm sorry, Anna. Are you all right?

– I'm fine. Where are you? I'll come and get you.

– I'm . . . I'm near a park. It's all right. Don't worry. I'll come home soon.

I stumble around the house, gathering the things I need. Laptop, clothes, photographs. I cannot concentrate. I am leaving behind not just a marriage, but a life. Why is this so hard when it is what I want to do? I leave my bags by the door. I call a cab.

I hear his key in the lock a second time. This time Paul does not smile and sweep me up in his arms. We stand and stare at each other.

He seems shrunken, shattered. How can I do this to someone? Is this what it is like to break up with a man? I have never broken off with anyone in my life. There was only one man before Paul, and he left me. Paul is all I have ever known.

– Deep down, I suppose I always knew your spirit would take you somewhere else.

– I do love you, sweetheart.

His face screws up in pain.

– Then please don't do this, baby. We can work it out. Please. We've been through so much together. You can't throw it all away.

Mark D'Arbanville

I stand at the crossroads of my life. I know if I stay now, I will never leave. Will I care for my pain, or for his?

I hold him and I feel like he is going to break. Why can't I just tell him I will stay, end his misery? Why am I being so fucking selfish? This is my life here, isn't it? He loves me and he needs me. What else do I need?

– Don't go, he whispers.

And I almost give in. Over his shoulder I see us smiling in our wedding photograph, and then I hear the cab sound its horn in the street outside. I push him away and pick up my bags. I have never felt more alone.

As I get in the cab I look back once over my shoulder through the window. He is standing in the doorway, slumped against the wall, and he is broken, quite broken. But then we are driving away. This is the first time in my life I have not gone back to rescue him, rescue anyone. Instead I have rescued me.

I cannot cry anymore. I am dry. I just have to do this, wash it all away, start again. I call Cathy. I ask her to tell everyone that I am leaving and that I will be in touch. She thinks I have left Paul to go to Mark, but I tell her the truth: from now on, it is just me. I don't much care if anyone thinks I am being selfish.

I stay at Sally's that night and the next morning I take a flight to Paris. I can lose myself there. A week later I rent a cottage near Reims, the capital of the Champagne region.

Ironic, I suppose. And somehow appropriate.

Ninety-two

And slowly, I start to heal.

My life is circumscribed by the rhythms of village life, a script I am writing, discovering things in myself that before I had only discovered and promoted in others. My nightmares are not as frequent. I woke one morning and the sadness that sometimes came on the bluest day was no longer there. It has not been there for a while now. Living alone is harder than I thought, it is more frightening and less certain than I had ever imagined. There are times I miss Paul very much.

But I want to move on with my life.

I bought an old 2CV. It rattles like a trolley bus, and trucks and Beemers honk in frustration when they pass me on the motorways. I have no DVD player, no credit card lunches, no power windows, but I am free.

Tonight I am driving down to Paris, a weekend in Paris on my own, to be me, to be free. I imagine I might dance at La Huchette.

I think of Mark as I drive, those eyes passionate and so blue, drinking me in, it is like a jolt of electricity runs through me. But then I remember his constant questioning of me, dissecting me, how I am two women, or three, how unhappy I make him when I don't do exactly as he wants.

He never knew me, he loved a version of me that he created in his head, his muse, his redemption, or whatever he thought I was. He wanted to make me his ideal, and I'm not that. I'm just a woman who made all these mistakes and was trying to work out who the hell she was.

Couldn't he just let it be? Couldn't he just accept me as I was, that second, that hour, whatever we had? Why do men and women have to love that way? Can't we accept each other as we are, without judging or trying to change them or make them better? Do we have to make them into something we want, something perhaps they don't want to be?

Yet there is something in Mark that I love, that I still love, that will never go away. We had not imagined this connection between us. If I saw him again, would it be possible to find true passionate crazy love with each other?

To finally have that spark ignite?

I would love to see him, just one more time, to find out.

Could he love me as I am, not as he imagined me?

Can you stand me anymore?

Can you just drink me tonight?

Ninety-three

A grey Parisian dawn, the city waking to the sound of traffic on the Rue Chateaudun. Condensation weeps down the window. Mark wipes the glass with his hand.

He had flown into Paris that morning to meet with his film producers, a French company negotiating for the rights to the script he had written with Anna. So much passion and pain in it, they said, too much for the Anglo-Saxon market. But the Latin temperament understood it better.

He has no idea if tomorrow will be a brighter day, and he doesn't want to send a false messenger. Rather not get his hopes set too high. Anna had found her answers; he had discovered that he could feel, then throttled the one woman who showed him how to do it. Not a good result, for him or the team.

He stays on in Paris an extra night. It is just impulse. He had heard from Sally that she is somewhere in France, and that night, from nostalgia or from hope, he walks along the

Mark D'Arbanville

Seine, stands on the Pont de Neuf where he had kissed her and where he had taken her photograph one cold morning. He smiles as he remembers her red nose and her demands for him to put his arm around her and make her toasty.

Never mind the Louvre! she had shouted. Where can we find a bar? I need champagne!

He eats dinner at a little restaurant on the Left Bank and then around ten o'clock his feet lead him inevitably towards one of the side streets close to the Notre Dame, a basement jazz club called La Huchette.

He pushes down the narrow and crowded stairs, then he stops and leans against the bare brick wall, watching.

She is there.

She is dancing with a Frenchman. Well, she would never be alone, this woman, not ever. She cannot dance, but he can, and he is leading her through the steps. Her hair has grown back and she is laughing and everyone is staring at the beautiful woman with the radiant smile and piercing blue eyes.

He watches her for a long time, dancing with one man after another, free at last. He thinks of going to her, asking her to dance, one more time. But he doesn't.

Instead he goes back up the stairs and walks home to his hotel.

Epilogue

Muxia, Galicia, Spain

Iglesia de Santa María de la Barca

Father Diego Calderón kneels before the Madonna. The breakers at the end of the earth throw themselves at the rocks below the iglesia. The votive candles flicker in the draught. He is alone tonight in the vaulted dark and he takes the prayer again from its place below the pedestal of the Virgin and says a prayer for the mysterious girl in the photograph, and the pilgrim who had brought her here.

He asks the Virgin for her intercession and to take the petition to her heart. For there are sometimes miracles in the world, of that he is sure. He reads the prayer printed on the back of the photograph, as he does every day at this time, for whoever this girl is, wherever she is now, whatever intercession she needs.

Mark D'Arbanville

. . . The miracle I pray for is that the clear blue innocent eyes you see in this photograph can be reinvented.

I pray that the energy light and passion for life can be reinvigorated and that the possibilities of life that were so fresh and reflected in these eyes will be returned and a sense of peace will remain.

I pray that the smile will return and be reflected by such inner happiness and hope that it will never leave this face again.

I pray that the inner turmoil will leave, the nightmares and cold sweats will fade away, and the inner child will heal.

And in its place a woman will emerge, with clear blue eyes, who can truly love and be loved.

This is my hope and this is the miracle I want for me.

Acknowledgments

I want to again thank my agent and friend Tim Curnow who knows the stories behind the stories and understands not only what a book is worth but what it can cost. Thank you; this book could not have got off the ground without you. I also want to thank my wonderful publisher at Random House, Jude McGee, for her support and faith in me. Thanks also at Random House to Peta Levett, my publicist, who put up with the Moodiest Author in the World during the birthing of this book. Thank you to Jo Jarrah for your wonderful editing. Thanks also to Lydia Papandrea, my senior editor, who cheerfully stretched the deadlines for me, found all the little holes I missed, and got me over the line. I would also like to say thank you to Random's wonderful marketing and sales team who got behind *The Naked Husband* because they believed in it, and not just because they had to. I would like also to thank the coincidentally named Anna Ross for her professional guidance on things I could not and cannot possibly understand. There are others whose contributions to *The Naked Heart* I would very much like to acknowledge but cannot, and I suppose that is what this book is all about.